The Buttaree Gudnis Affair: Murder in Waikiki

Archie and Kimo Hawaiian Tales #1

Chet Novicki

Table of Contents

Chapter One

Tuesday, 3:07 A.M. HST (Hawaii Standard Time)

The circumstances of my initial meeting with Buttaree Gudnis were, to put it mildly, highly unusual. For one thing, it happened at three o'clock on a Tuesday morning. The time actually wasn't so out of the ordinary for me – I work nights and ordinarily don't get home until after two. It was the second part of our meeting that put it into the category of 'highly unusual.' She was naked. Like, completely, totally, 100% without clothes of any kind. Oh, and she was also dripping wet.

Let me tell you what happened.

I was sitting on my living room couch, watching TV with the sound off, just relaxing with a beer after another boring night at my crap-ass job out by the airport, when my reverie was disturbed by a soft knocking at my apartment door. A quick look through the peephole revealed the previously-mentioned Buttaree Gudnis. Now, I'm a fairly cautious guy. I have a bit of an anxiety issue and am not known to be the *trusting* sort. And I normally wouldn't open my door to a stranger in the middle of the night, but this situation was, well, different – she was naked. I opened the door, ignoring that little voice in my head that was telling me to ... *Be careful.*

"Hi. I'm Buttaree," she said. "I just moved in across the hall a couple of days ago." She glanced nervously across the hall at the open door to her apartment while she dripped water onto the hallway floor, creating a small puddle.

"Yeah, I saw you moving in," I said, checking her out. Technically, I guess, she wasn't totally naked. She had a small – very small – blue towel in one hand and was using it to cover her pubic region, while her other arm was folded across her breasts, blocking my view of her nipples.

"I think someone's in my apartment – in my bedroom. Can I come in?"

Not wanting to appear unneighborly to an apparent damsel in distress, I held open my door and she came in, transferring her puddle-producing proclivities from the hallway to my living room carpet.

"Uh, let me get you a towel," I said, and disappeared into my bedroom, emerging in short order with two towels, an old, long-sleeve dress shirt, and a pair of boxer shorts that hadn't fit me since I was a teenager. "Here, you can put these on." I laid them all over the back of a chair and turned away.

"Thanks."

Remembering my manners, I introduced myself while keeping my back to her. "I'm Archie. Archie Morris," I told her, at the same time watching her reflection in my living room mirror as she dried herself off and got dressed. Maybe 24 or 25 years old, not too tall, medium-length blonde hair and a very attractive body. Nice looking girl, I decided.

When she'd finished dressing, she tapped me on the shoulder and I turned back around to face her. "Buttaree Gudnis," she said, extending her hand for me to shake.

I shook her hand. "Buttery Goodness. That's an unusual name."

She spelled it for me. "My father's little joke on his poor, helpless, newborn babies – giving them funny names. When I was a little girl, he told me that when I grew up I was going to marry a man named Mr. Gracious, and then I'd be Buttaree Gudnis Gracious. I also have a sister named Lemonee and a brother named Omai." She spelled those for me, too.

Buttaree, Lemonee, and Omai Gudnis. Cute. "So, what's going on in your apartment?" I said.

"I think there's someone in my bedroom. I just got out of the shower and I heard noises in there."

"Maybe it's someone you know. And they're just waiting for you to get out of the shower," I suggested.

"In my bedroom? I don't think so. Besides, I don't really know anyone here in Honolulu. I just moved here last month."

"Well, ..."

"You wanna go check?" she said. "The two of us, I mean. I'll go with you."

"Uh, not really. They could have a gun or something." As I mentioned earlier, I'm normally a fairly cautious guy. Plus, I have that little issue with anxiety. Here in my apartment, where I felt safe and secure, it was never much of a problem, but if I went snooping around, looking for a burglar, I'm pretty sure it would be. "How about I call the police and get them to check?"

"The police? Well ... yeah, okay, I guess."

I turned off the TV, grabbed my phone and called 911. "Have a seat," I said, motioning toward my couch.

Buttaree sat on my couch and watched as I explained our situation to the operator. When I was finished, she said, "And?"

"They're sending someone right over to check it out," I said.

"Great," she said in a less-than-enthusiastic voice, and then added, "I guess," as an afterthought.

"You don't like cops?"

"They're okay, some of them."

Talking about the police didn't seem to be Buttaree's favorite topic of conversation, so I changed the subject. "How about a beer?"

"Sure. I'd love one."

I picked up my almost-empty beer from the coffee table and drained it as I went into the kitchen. "You want a glass?" I called, grabbing two Coronas from the fridge and heading back into the living room.

"No. Bottle's fine."

"Good. I don't think I have any clean glasses," I said as I handed her a Corona and sat down on the couch next to her.

She grinned, revealing nice, straight, Hollywood-white teeth, maybe her best feature. "Just like me," she said. Then, still grinning, she raised her beer toward me and offered a toast. "Here's to meeting new people."

"In unusual ways," I added, clinking my bottle against hers.

"Yes." She glanced over at my door, probably wondering what was going on over at her place. "In unusual ways."

We sat in silence for a minute or so, drinking our beers, until finally Buttaree said, "So, what do you do, Archie? How come you're still up at this time of night?"

"Oh, I have a part-time job working nights out by the airport, packing up stuff Asian tourists buy. They ship it out to Asia on an early-morning flight."

"Part time?"

"Yeah. I work from eight at night until two in the morning, four days a week."

"And that's it? That's your only job?"

"Yeah."

"How do you survive working just part time? Honolulu's gotta be one of the most expensive cities in the country to live in. Maybe in the entire world. Are you rich?"

"Yeah, I'm rich," I said, laughing at the same time so she'd know I was kidding.

"I'm serious," she said.

"Well, I thought I was rich, once upon a time. I own this apartment, for example. It's not much, but it's paid for – all I have to pay is the maintenance fee and taxes. I inherited it from a great-aunt I only met a few times in my life. She was from Boston and she used to come over here in the winter to escape the cold."

"That was nice of her. To leave you the apartment, I mean."

"Yeah, it was. I think it's because I was named after her – we have the same first name. And it's not Archie, by the way. She also left me a chunk of cash – over a hundred thousand dollars – and that old Chevy that's parked down in the garage."

"Wow," Buttaree said, taking a sip of her beer and looking suitably impressed. "So, if it's not Archie, what is your real first name?"

I paused. Revealing my first name was not something I took lightly. "Meredith," I said. "My full name is Meredith Archibald Morris."

Buttaree giggled. "That's kind of an odd name."

"And this is coming from someone named Buttaree Gudnis?"

Her giggle relaxed into a smile. "Right. I see your point."

"Her name was Meredith Belknap Tilton-Franklin," I said.

"You know, you can tell she had money just from her name," Buttaree observed.

"I guess. Anyway, I thought I was rich. I had wheels, my own apartment, and cash. I was 24 years old and ready to party. And I did, too. But that was then, three or four years ago, and this is now."

"What's different now?"

"Most of the money's gone, for one thing."

"Bummer."

"I agree." I took a long pull on my beer and checked my watch. Three-thirty. The police should be here pretty soon. "So I'm going to have to start looking for a real job. One that offers full-time hours and health insurance, you know."

"That sucks. Job hunting, I mean."

"Yeah, I'm not looking forward to it. But it's not something I have to do tomorrow. I'm still good for a couple of more months. Maybe even 'til the end of the year."

"Well, good luck."

"Thanks. So, what do you do, Buttaree? What brings you to Honolulu?"

"I'm a dancer."

"A dancer?"

"Uh-huh. I got a job at Busteroo's."

"You mean, uh ... that strip club down on Kapiolani Boulevard?"

"Yup, that's the one. I dance there six nights a week. Naked."

"What?"

"Naked. I dance naked." She said it without embarrassment, as if dancing naked was as normal as being a nurse or a secretary. Personally, I'd be a little reluctant to admit it if I were a naked dancer, but I suppose that's just me. Or maybe I'd feel different if I were in better shape, but I'm – what's a nice way to put this? – just a little on the pleasantly pudgy side. I really need to start getting some exercise.

"I hear you guys – exotic dancers, I mean – make a lot of money. Is that true?"

"Yup. It's ridiculous, really. I come out wearing nothing but high heels and a gold chain around my waist, and all the gynecologists lean forward and get real serious, you know. Then I wiggle around a little bit and show 'em my stuff and they throw money at me. Lots of money. It's great." She chuckled, apparently at the thought of all that money being thrown at her.

"Gynecologists? What, is there a convention or something in town?"

Her chuckle turned into a laugh. "No. No convention. That's what we call those guys who sit right at the front of the stage and really, really, really concentrate on watching you dance. They specialize in watching a certain part of your anatomy, if you know what I mean. So, gynecologists is what we call 'em."

I couldn't think of any good reply to that surprising piece of news so I took a sip of my beer and said, "Interesting. I never knew that." Even more surprising, at least to me, was the subject matter we'd been discussing. Most of the time, when I meet a girl for the first time, we don't end up talking about her anatomy and what guys who stare at it are called.

"You should come see me dance, sometime," she said.

Before I could respond to Buttaree's invitation, my doorbell rang. I hopped off the couch and crossed to the door, leaving the invite hanging in the air. A quick peek through the peephole confirmed what I suspected. "It's the cops," I announced, and opened the door.

Chapter Two

There were two of them, each wearing the summertime Waikiki police uniform of shorts and white, short-sleeve shirts. Here in Waikiki they ride around on bicycles, reminding tourists not to jaywalk or litter. Although I'm not 100% sure, I suppose that in other, larger areas of Honolulu, they let them use cars and wear long pants.

"Mr. Morris?" said the taller of the two, a blonde, freckle-faced *haole* about my age.

"Yeah, that's me. C'mon in." I held the door open wide and stepped aside to let them enter.

"I'm Officer Jenkins," the haole cop said. "This is my partner, Officer Cabacungan."

I shook hands with each of them, although I'm not certain you're required to do that. Officer Cabacungan was about the same age as his Caucasian partner, but a dark bronze color and much shorter. And even though Cabacungan is a Filipino name, he looked Japanese. That's the way it is in Hawaii these days – you can no longer tell people's ethnicity from their names or the way they look. There's been too much intermarriage among the various ethnic groups that make up the state, and the population has become a jumble of people who identify as Japanese-Chinese-Hawaiian or Korean-Haole-Samoan, or something similar. Even I fall into this group. Although I look 100% haole, what with my brown hair and light skin color, I'm actually 50% Japanese.

"So, what seems to be the problem?" Officer Jenkins said.

Buttaree popped up from the couch and joined us by the door. "It's actually my problem," she told Officer Jenkins.

"Ma'am?" he said.

"I think someone is in my apartment – or was in my apartment. I live right across the hall."

"You mean an intruder?" said Officer Cabacungan.

"Yeah. I was taking a shower, and I heard these noises in my bedroom. Like someone opening and closing dresser drawers, you know. So I came over here and we called you guys."

"Right across the hall?" said Officer Jenkins. "All right. We'll go check it out for you. You wanna let us in?"

"The door's not locked – I don't think I even closed it tight."

"Okay, we'll take a look and then come back and tell you what we found."

I let the two cops out and left the door open. "It's that one. Right there," Buttaree called after them, pointing at her apartment. Officer Jenkins gave us a little wave of his hand without looking back.

We sat back down on the couch to await the return of Officers Jenkins and Cabacungan. "You want another beer while we wait?" I said.

"No, I'm good." She looked thoughtful, gazing off into the distance as if she had something important on her mind.

"Penny for your thoughts," I said.

She turned toward me and smiled. "I think maybe I'm just being paranoid, you know. There's probably no one in my apartment at all. It's just ..." Her voice trailed off.

"Just what?"

"Just, ... there's this guy – this really creepy-looking old guy – and I think ... well, I don't know what I think. But I've been working at Busteroo's for about three weeks now, and before I found this apartment I was staying at an apartment-hotel down at the other end of Waikiki, you know. And there was this guy who used to hang out in front and look up at my place a lot. There's a bus stop there and he used to just sit on the bench, like he was waiting for the bus, but he never got on when the bus stopped." She paused to finish her beer in one long gulp.

"Uh-huh," I said. "So ... ?"

"I'm pretty sure I saw this same guy at the club a couple of times, and he was, like, watching me but trying to pretend he wasn't. You know?"

"Well, isn't that why guys go to clubs like Busteroo's – to see naked girls? It could be he's just shy," I offered.

"Yeah. Or he could be a psycho killer."

"Let's hope not."

"But there's more. Tonight, when the taxi was bringing me home, I thought I saw him again, just down the street, on Kuhio, walking this way."

"Are you sure it's the same guy? Maybe it's just a couple of different guys who look alike."

"Maybe. But I don't think so."

"What's he look like?"

"He's old. Gray hair and a big, bushy, gray mustache. And the reason I think it's the same guy is because he's always wearing the same clothes – shorts, a mostly-blue aloha shirt, and a blue baseball cap. Oh, and rubber zoris – no shoes. He's a white guy, I think, but he's really tan."

"You should tell all this to the cops when they come back."

"I don't think so," Buttaree said, without further explanation.

"Well, if I see him hanging around, I'll ask him what he's doing. How's that?"

"That sounds great. Maybe threaten him a little," she said with a little chuckle. "Tell him I've got a great big boyfriend who's part of the local mafia or something. There is a local mafia, I assume."

"Yeah. Not the Mafia mafia, but local organized crime. We've got that. There's a rumor they own the club where you work."

"Busteroo's?"

"Yeah."

"I'm not surprised. You should see some of the creeps who work there. Guys, I mean – not the dancers. Definitely mob types."

A light tapping on my open door announced the return of Officers Jenkins and Cabacungan from their inspection of Buttaree's apartment. "Come on in," I called as she and I rose to greet them.

"Was anybody there?" Buttaree said.

"No, ma'am," said Officer Cabacungan.

Officer Jenkins shot a slightly-peeved look in the direction of his partner, as if to imply that he should be the only one engaged in this conversation, and said, "We searched the place quite thoroughly and didn't find anyone or anything that would indicate someone was there. However, ..."

"Yes?" said Buttaree.

"I, uh, don't want to embarrass you or anything – "

"Don't worry about it. I'm not easily embarrassed."

"The bedroom was pretty messy. Things were scattered about and we couldn't really tell if an intruder did that or if – "

"That was me. I just moved in a couple of days ago and I was having trouble finding things. Clothes, I mean. So I was just, kinda, you know, tossing things around, looking for stuff."

"I see. Well, anyway, it's safe for you to return to your apartment. If anyone was in there, he's gone now. Also, we closed your door but we didn't lock it."

"That's good," she said. "I don't have my keys." She thanked the two officers and waved goodbye to them as they left.

"They were pretty nice," I said as I closed my door.

"Yeah, not bad at all. For cops."

I got the distinct impression Buttaree had experienced less-pleasant encounters with cops, somewhere along the way. But her history with the police was really none of my business, and I didn't pursue the subject. "So ... ?" I said.

"Yeah, I've gotta get going," she said. "I really appreciate this, Archie – you helping me and all. I was like totally freaking out and you saved me." She leaned over and kissed me on the cheek.

It was a friendly, thank you type of kiss – nothing romantic about it, but for a brief moment I had the idea that I should invite her to spend the rest of the night with me, where she'd be safe from anyone intending her harm. I decided against it, though, which was probably a good thing. Hitting on a neighbor in distress would have been just a little bit creepy. Instead, I opened the door to let her leave.

"I'll get your clothes back to you after I wash them," she said.

"Sure. No hurry. They don't fit me anymore, anyway."

I waited in my doorway as she crossed to her apartment, opened the door and went inside, giving me a smile and one of those little finger-waves as she closed her door. Then I closed and locked my own door and got ready for bed, thinking totally inappropriate thoughts about my new neighbor.

Chapter Three

Two nights later, at about the same time as when I'd first met her, Buttaree reappeared at my front door. This time, however, when I opened the door, she was dry, fully clothed, and carrying a bucket of fried chicken and a six-pack of beer. She smiled at me and said, "Hungry?"

"Always," I said, letting her in.

"Just my way of saying thanks for the other night." She held up the beer and chicken for me to see.

"Here, let me get that." I put the chicken on the coffee table, along with two of the beers, and went into the kitchen, returning with two plates and a roll of paper towels.

"Let's eat," Buttaree said, plopping herself down on my couch.

"So, tough night?" I said, taking a piece of chicken from the bucket and passing the bucket over to her.

"Nah." She took a sip of her beer and grabbed a piece of chicken. "Good night, actually. The gynos were really generous tonight. One of them even threw a couple of twenties at me."

"He must be rich. Maybe he wants to meet you."

"Yeah, maybe. You know, I don't get it."

"Get what?"

"These guys. Some of them are in the club almost every night, throwing money at the girls. I don't know why they don't just hire a hooker instead of wasting all that cash."

"I guess some guys just like to look," I said. "Or maybe they're afraid of prostitutes."

"Yeah, I guess. How much do hookers charge, anyway, here in Hawaii?"

"I don't really know. I've never, uh, hired one."

Buttaree gave me a *Really?* look and bit into a drumstick.

"But I've heard it's tourist prices," I continued. "Like, several hundred dollars for one of those tall blondes you see walking up and down Kalakaua Avenue late at night."

"Several hundred dollars? That's ridiculous!"

"I agree."

"Down where I come from, hookers charge about $50 or $60. And you can get a quickie blowjob for a twenty-dollar bill."

I almost choked on my chicken when Buttaree said that, and I didn't want to ask her how she knew so much about this subject, so instead I said, "Where is that, anyway? Where are you from?"

"Florida. Avon Park, Florida."

"Never heard of it."

"I'm not surprised. It's a little town in the central part of the state, just north of Sebring."

"I've never been to Florida," I said. "Actually, I've never even been to the mainland."

"What? You've never been to the mainland?"

"That's right. Born and raised here, never been anywhere else except to a couple of the neighbor islands."

"Wow, you're like a travel virgin. Since I left home, I've been all over." She reeled off a list of about a dozen cities, ending with, "– and just before I came here, Los Angeles."

"That's a pretty impressive list," I said.

"It's the business. The clubs like to have a steady supply of new dancers, you know. So we're constantly moving from club to club, from city to city. Six months in one city, three or four months someplace else. Always moving."

"I don't know if I'd like that or not. Always moving, I mean."

"Yeah, it can be kinda tiring, trying to get settled in a new place every four or five months, finding a place to stay, all those kinds of minor hassles."

"I suppose so."

"But in some ways it's great. I've been dancing for about five years now, and I've been all over the country. Seen places I never would have seen, otherwise. Like Cheyenne, Wyoming – I spent four months there. That's a place I probably never would have visited if I wasn't a dancer."

We continued eating in silence. After several minutes, Buttaree threw a half-eaten piece of chicken onto her plate, wiped her hands on a paper towel, drained her beer and said, "That's it for me. I've gotta go – I have an appointment at ten and I wanna get a little sleep, at least."

"Well, thanks for the chow. And the company, too. I enjoyed both."

She smiled. "Me, too. We can do it again, if you want."

"Sure, anytime. I'm always around, this time of night."

"Great." She stood up and pointed at her plate. "Should I put this in the kitchen?"

"No, leave it. I'll get it." I started to get up.

"Relax," she said. "I can let myself out."

"What about your beer? And the rest of this chicken?"

"Keep it." She started toward the door, then halfway there turned and said, "You know, I like you a lot, Archie. You're a nice guy."

I laughed. "Not just nice, I'm *really* nice," I corrected her.

She laughed back, blew me a kiss and was out the door, locking it as she left.

After Buttaree's departure, I got myself another beer and flopped back down onto my couch, assuming my normal position – deep slouch, bare feet on the edge of the coffee table. I was confused and I had some serious thinking to do.

First off, what the hell was going on? With me and Buttaree, I mean. Was she interested in me? Maybe as a short-term boyfriend for a couple of months? That seemed more than a little hard to believe because I definitely am not the stripper-boyfriend type – girls I've dated in the past have always had jobs that required them to wear clothes. Still, it was a little odd the way she'd just popped by with food and drink, even if ostensibly it was to thank me for rescuing her from a non-existent intruder. And then she'd told me we could do this again, if that's what I wanted. That sounded as if she wanted to spend more time with me.

And I liked girls. A lot. All kinds of girls. That included Buttaree – I liked her. She was fun and interesting and good-looking. But I've always been a little on the shy side around women and, because of Buttaree's job, I was a little leery of becoming involved with her. Basically, she was a sex worker and I knew that business was populated by a lot of sleazy people with whom I didn't want to become acquainted. I've always tried to stay away from those kind of people, although long ago I used to buy weed from a guy who had a particularly skanky-looking girlfriend and I always wondered what her story was.

This whole thing with Buttaree was puzzling. Was I reading the situation correctly? Maybe I had it all wrong and she was just lonely and wanted someone to talk to, and I was always conveniently nearby. After all, she was new in town and she'd said she didn't know anyone here.

I sat there, drinking my beer and pondering my problem, unable to come to a decision. Maybe I should ask her if she wanted to do something during the day, when we were both free, I thought. We could go to the beach or a movie or I could show her around the island. That last part – showing her the local sights – sounded like a good approach. After all, I had a car and she didn't, and I could casually suggest, "Hey, Buttaree, how about I show you around our beautiful island one of these days?" She'd probably be up for something like that.

Or, I could forget about all of that and just wait and see if anything was going to happen. I was pretty sure Buttaree would let me know if she had any romantic plans for the two of us. That really sounded like the best plan, I decided – probably because it removed the decision-making process from me and placed it on her. It also eliminated any chance I might make a complete fool of myself because of a total misunderstanding of our relationship.

So, with the decision made and a plan firmly in mind, I finished my beer, cleaned up the living room, and got ready for bed.

Chapter Four

On Saturday afternoon, my best friend, Kimo, came over. We got together almost every Saturday – once upon a time it was to go to the park and play basketball, but more recently it was just to sit around and drink beer and smoke weed and watch sports on TV. And talk about girls.

We used to dominate games at the park. At roughly six feet seven inches tall and a pretty mobile 300-plus pounds, Kimo was bigger than just about anyone we ever encountered, and a lot more skillful than most. And he used to take full advantage of both his height and his bulk to dominate those pickup games. The best part of all this was, even though I was just barely six feet tall and not that great a player, as his best friend, I was always on his team.

But then, a couple of years ago, his knees started to ache, and his doctor advised him to lose weight and to quit playing basketball. And so we quit playing sports in favor of watching them on TV.

Kimo's real name was William Tadashi Lihikaiulani, which always struck me as a little strange since Kimo is the Hawaiian name for James or Jimmy, not William. But back when I first met him – when he transferred into the third grade at Waikiki Elementary School – he introduced himself as Kimo and he's been Kimo ever since. He told me his Hawaiian grandmother gave him the name because 'he looked like a Kimo,' and he needed a nice Hawaiian name. The Hawaiian name for William is Wiliama, which she said was just a haole name spelled funny and wouldn't do for someone who looked like a Kimo.

Many of the other kids in our class – heck, in our school – were a little afraid of him because he was so big. He was nearly twice the size of anyone in our class, which was made up largely of kids from the local Kapahulu neighborhood, an area heavily populated by families of Asian descent. In other words, many of our classmates were small in stature. But Kimo took after the Hawaiian side of his family, and even for a Polynesian, who tend to be a large people, he was huge.

We became friends about two minutes after we met. I went up to him at recess and said, "Hey, howzit?" which is a friendly greeting, locally. "I'm Archie."

"Hey, Archie. Howzit?" he said. "Kimo."

"What?" I said, not understanding what he meant. The teacher had introduced him to the class as William and, as I said, Kimo was the Hawaiian name for James, not William.

"Kimo," he repeated. "I'm Kimo. Everyone calls me Kimo."

"Okay. Kimo." And then, getting right to the point, I said, "Are you half Japanese?"

"Yeah, I am. How did you know?"

"When Mrs. Nakamura introduced you to the class, she said your middle name was Tadashi. That's Japanese."

"So?"

"Me, too. I'm half Japanese, too."

"Yeah? You look like one haole."

"I know. But my mother's Japanese."

"Mine, too."

And that was the beginning of our friendship. Over time, our mothers became friends, too. And then our fathers, although to a lesser degree. Eventually we became something like a blended family, with me spending half my time growing up at the Lihikaiulani house and Kimo spending an almost-equal amount of time at my house.

He was standing there, holding a 12-pack and a giant bag of pretzels, when I opened the door to my apartment. "Howdy hi," he said.

"Daddy brings goodies." He grinned and held up the beer and pretzels for me to see, then breezed past me and went straight into the kitchen.

I closed the door and resumed my seat on the couch, where I'd been semi-snoozing. "I'm glad you brought beer," I called to him. "I'm almost out."

He joined me on the couch, plopping a cold Corona onto the table in front of me. "Not only beer. I brought this." He pulled out a bag of buds and handed it over to me.

I opened the baggie and stuck my nose in the bag, taking a big whiff. "Wow, nice. Where'd you get this? And how much?"

"You know Donna?" he said.

"I don't think so."

"She's that secretary who works for Dr. Kamm. Or maybe she's a receptionist, I'm not sure. I met her a couple of weeks ago – I thought I told you about her."

"Yeah, maybe. But I guess I forgot." It was easy to forget the names of Kimo's female friends – it seemed he had a new girlfriend every other week. He was, as he liked to remind me from time to time, a *beeg-time playah*.

"Anyway, she's crazy about me and her brother's a grower. She gave me this weed as a present."

"Wow, that's impressive. There's probably a couple of hundred bucks worth of stuff here. She must really like you."

"Yeah. And that ain't all. Look." He pulled three joints out of his shirt pocket, tossed two of them onto the coffee table and stuck the third in his mouth, lighting it and taking a long hit.

"Hey! What about me?" I said when he failed to pass me the joint.

He exhaled, took another long hit and passed the joint over. "I'm testing it," he managed to squeeze out without exhaling.

I conducted my own test, and within a couple of minutes of passing the joint back and forth, I had a nice buzz. "This is some good shit," I said, grinning at Kimo.

He grinned back. "Yeah, smooth. Not harsh. Stony, too."

"Yeah."

We sat in silence for a couple of minutes, taking turns with the joint and sucking on our beers, absorbing our highs and enjoying that comfortable warm feeling that slowly envelops the back part of your brain. At least, that's what I was doing – I assumed Kimo was having a similar experience.

"How's your folks?" I said.

"They're good."

"Business?"

"That's good, too."

Kimo's dad was a retired Honolulu cop – a captain, I think, although I never really paid much attention to the HPD rank system. Anyway, after he retired he started a security firm and made Kimo his first hire. It was basically just a rent-a-cop operation, but nearly all of the employees were ex-cops picking up a little extra cash to supplement their pensions, and it soon developed into a successful business. And since Kimo's dad spent most days down at the police station, hanging out with his old buddies, Kimo pretty much ran the whole show. Not a bad gig for a pot-smoking, woman-chasing *playah*, in my opinion.

"So how are your folks?" he said.

"Okay, I guess. Actually, I haven't seen them for a while."

"Yeah? How come?"

"I dunno, just busy, I guess. I've been meaning to go down to the store and check in, but just haven't got around to it." My folks own a small, tourist-trap kind of store here in Waikiki.

"It's your dad," Kimo said.

"What?"

"Your dad. You're just afraid he's gonna rag on you. You know, get a better job, go back to school, make something of yourself. Do something! Like that."

"He's not there in the mornings. He plays golf at Ala Wai. It's just my mom."

"So go then. In the morning."

"Yeah." I struggled to my feet from my semi-reclined position. "Want another beer?"

He took a long swig and handed me his empty bottle. "Bring the pretzels, too."

When I was back on the couch with fresh beers and the pretzels, I said, "I met a girl."

Kimo's eyebrows shot up in mock surprise. "Really?" he said in an exaggerated tone.

"Yup."

"What's her name? Is she local?"

"She's from Florida. Buttaree Gudnis."

"That's a helluva name for a town," he said, laughing.

"No, that's *her* name. Not the town she's from."

He laughed even harder. "You're kidding me. What is it, again? Buttery Goodness?"

I spelled Buttaree's name for him. He was halfway into a large swallow of beer when I told him she had a sister named Lemonee and her brother's name was Omai, causing him to choke with laughter.

"Don't do that," he said when he'd recovered.

"Sorry," I said, but I was laughing as I said it.

"So how'd you meet her?"

"She moved into the apartment across the hall. Where the Changs used to live."

"That's convenient. Have you taken her out?"

"Not exactly." I went on to explain the situation with Buttaree – how we'd met under unusual circumstances, how she'd dropped by with the chicken and beer to thank me, and how she'd suggested we should get together again.

"Interesting," Kimo said when I'd finished. "She's a stripper, huh?"

"A nude dancer."

"Same thing. There aren't any real strippers anymore. Since they all start out naked, there's nothing to take off."

"So whaddaya think?"

"About what?" Kimo retrieved the half-smoked joint from the ashtray and lit it, taking a deep hit and then passing it to me.

"About me and her." I took a hit and put the joint back in the ashtray.

"Go for it, dude. That's my advice. Always. Just go for it."

"You think?"

"That's what I'd do. Go for it."

"Okay, then."

"Anyway, I gotta split," Kimo said.

"Already? You just got here."

He gave me a funny look. "It's been about three hours, dude."

I checked my watch. Sure enough, we'd been sitting on my couch, just talking, drinking beer and smoking weed for almost exactly three hours. Weed will do that to you, sometimes. Cause time distortion, I mean. "Time flies when you're having fun," I said.

Kimo stood up to leave. "That's for you," he said, pointing at the bag of weed on my coffee table.

"You're kidding," I said, getting to my feet.

"No. Donna gave me about a quarter-pound. That's just some of it. I've still got plenty."

"Shoots, man, thanks. I'll make good use of it, I'm sure."

"Share some of it with your new sweetie," he said, laughing, and with a wave of his hand, he was gone.

I lit up the one remaining joint – evidently we'd smoked two joints when I thought we'd only smoked one, since there were two roaches in the ashtray – and took several hits, then closed my eyes and let my thoughts wander away to Buttaree. Kimo was right. I should just 'go for it.' But slowly. Just go for it, but slowly.

Chapter Five

A couple of days went by before I saw Buttaree again. It was around noon and she was getting out of the elevator as I was about to get on, so I stopped to chat, letting the elevator leave without me.

"Getting settled in?" I said.

"Yeah. It's a pain in the ass, moving."

"I'll bet."

"Fortunately, I travel light. Got to, in this business."

"I suppose so."

"I've been meaning to come over and see you," she said.

"Really? Something wrong?"

"No, just to hang out, shoot the shit. Maybe have a couple of beers."

"Sure. Come on over anytime."

"I did see that guy again, though. This morning."

"Guy?"

"You know, that old guy I told you about. With the shorts and aloha shirt."

"Oh, yeah. Where'd you see him?"

"He was sitting on that rock wall across the street when I left to go shopping," she said, indicating a bag of groceries she'd set down beside her. "And when he saw me coming down the walk to the street, he left, heading up that way." She pointed in the general direction of Ala Wai Boulevard.

"Maybe he lives around here and that's why you keep seeing him."

"I doubt it. I saw him down at my old place and at the club a couple of times, and I even saw him once at Ala Moana Shopping Center. I was

24

going up the escalator by that big courtyard and he was standing up at the top, just staring down at me."

"Yeah? What happened?"

"Nothing. I looked away and when I looked back he was gone. And when I got to the second floor he wasn't there."

"Strange," I said.

"Yeah, strange," Buttaree agreed.

"Well, I'll keep an eye out for him and if I see him I'll ask him what's going on."

"Thanks." She leaned over and picked up her shopping bag, which I took to be a signal our conversation was over. "I think he might be a stalker. That's one of the hazards of this business, you know."

"I didn't know that." I wasn't sure what to think about Buttaree's stalker, if that's what he was. He could be just a fan with a crush, or maybe he didn't even exist – I hadn't seen him. Or perhaps Buttaree was being paranoid. I supposed it wouldn't be that unusual for girls in the nude dancing business to suffer from a bit of paranoia. In fact, it might be unusual if they didn't have paranoid thoughts from time to time, what with all the creeps they were bound to run into.

"You gonna be around tonight?" she said.

"After work."

"Maybe I'll come over, then."

"Sure."

"Don't eat – I'll bring us something."

"Okay."

"And some beer."

"I've got plenty of beer," I said.

"Great. Just food, then." She turned and headed off toward her apartment. "Toodles," she called over her shoulder.

"See you tonight," I called after her.

It was almost three when Buttaree knocked on my door. I was watching an old movie from the thirties – a mystery with tons of British actors in it – and having trouble understanding what they were saying, so I had the sound turned up pretty high. Buttaree commented on it when I let her in.

"You have hearing problems?" she said when I opened the door.

"No. Why?"

"I could hear your TV in the elevator."

"Really? I better turn it down." I went over to the couch and began a search for my always-elusive remote. "What's in the bag?" I said, indicating the plastic bag she'd placed on my coffee table.

"Plate lunches."

"What kind?"

"All kinds."

I found the remote and turned the volume on the TV down to a more-reasonable level. "Whaddaya mean, 'all kinds?'"

"There's steak and chicken and a pork cutlet and macaroni salad and, like, four scoops of rice on each plate."

"Really? Where'd you get that at this time of night?"

"I made it," she said.

"What?"

"I made it. At work. In the kitchen. They serve food at the club, you know."

"I didn't know that."

"Yeah. Something to do with the liquor license. If they serve food they can stay open later."

I wasn't quite sure how I felt about eating food that came from a strip-club kitchen, but I went into the kitchen, grabbed a couple of beers from the fridge and some real knives and forks – plate lunches always come with wimpy plastic utensils or maybe just chopsticks – and joined Buttaree on the couch in the living room.

She removed the aluminum foil from one of the plate lunches and passed it over to me. It was enormous – easily the largest plate lunch I'd ever seen in my life, and I've seen thousands. Plate lunches are a way of life here in Hawaii.

I put the paper plate on my lap and set out to reduce the giant mountain of food on it down to a more reasonable size, like a hill or a smaller mountain. There was no way I could eat that much food in one sitting. "I'll be eating on this for days," I said.

"Me, too." She eyed the pile of food on her own plate. "I might have got carried away a little bit," she said with a smile.

"So how's work? Everything okay?"

"I saw that guy again. The old guy. He was in the club, sitting with a couple of hoods."

"Hoods?"

"You know, gangsters, bad guys, like that."

"How do you know that's what they were?"

"Well, I don't know for sure, but that's what they looked like. Like mobsters. From the mainland, though – not local. They were dressed real fancy, wearing those shiny suits like they wear. I've seen plenty of those kinds of guys since I've been doing this job. On the mainland, I mean."

"But they're not hassling you or anything, right?"

"No, but they kept watching me and then leaning forward to talk to each other and then watching me some more, over and over."

I laughed. "C'mon, Buttaree, you're a nude dancer. Guys are gonna look at you. That's why they're in the club – to see naked girls."

She took a giant swig of her beer, washing down a mouthful of steak and macaroni salad. "I know," she said, dabbing at her mouth with one of about two dozen napkins she'd brought along. "But this was different. I've seen lots of guys watching me since I've been doing this. They watch and then they talk to their friends, but it's always kinda light and humorous, you know. Sometimes they're even laughing – I always wonder what they're saying, if they're making jokes about me, about the way I look."

"I doubt that. You look fine."

She smiled over at me. "But these guys were different. Whatever they were talking about, it was really serious."

My mouth was full of food, so I nodded and grunted to show I understood.

"You know what I thought?" Buttaree said.

I shook my head.

"That maybe they were planning to kidnap me."

I swallowed my food and said, "I think you're probably just being paranoid. That kinda stuff only happens in the movies."

"Oh, no. A girl like me – young, blonde, nice body – can be sold for a fortune in some countries. I've heard stories."

"Really?"

"Yup. So I've been told." She put her plate of food on the table and leaned back. "I'm full."

I looked at her plate – she'd taken about two bites.

She saw me looking and said, "We dancers have to watch our weight, you know."

I responded by taking two large bites of my food and then taking both of our plates into the kitchen, returning with the bag of weed Kimo had given me. "Check this out," I said, showing it to her.

"Wow! Weed. I love weed."

"Doesn't everyone?" I lit up one of several joints I'd rolled earlier and passed it over, watching as she took a long hit and held it. Obviously an experienced smoker, I told myself.

"What are we watching, here, anyway?" she said, exhaling and indicating the TV with her hand.

"I don't know. Some old movie from long ago. Want me to turn it off?"

"No. Turn the sound up a little and let's see what's going on."

I turned up the volume and we sat back, watching in silence for several minutes, passing the joint back and forth.

"This is great," Buttaree said, pointing at the bag of weed on the coffee table. "Really good shit."

"Yeah. Best thing is, it was free. My friend, Kimo, gave it to me."

"Wow, nice friend."

"Yeah. I'll give you some to take with you."

"No need. I'll just come over here and smoke with you, if that's okay." She smiled at me.

"Sure. Anytime."

"You don't mind me coming over here all the time like this?"

"Not a bit. I enjoy your company."

"Great." She turned her attention back to the TV. "So what's going on here? Do you know? What's he doing with that soap?"

I paused the TV while I attempted to catch her up on the movie's storyline. "I missed the beginning. But that guy there on the screen just killed a guy and stole a bag of diamonds from him. Then he hid the diamonds in a locker. That's about when you got here."

"So what's with the soap? Why is he carving it?"

"I'm not sure. But you see that key on the table there?" I pointed at the left side of the screen, where you could see a small key sitting on a kitchen table. "That's the key to the locker where he hid the diamonds. I think he's trying to make a hole in the soap so he can hide the key inside it."

"Sure is taking him a long time."

"Soap's hard," I said.

"Yeah. He should have picked something soft. Like butter."

"Butter?"

"Sure. Take out a new stick of butter and carefully unwrap it but leave it sitting on the wrapper. Wait for the butter to get soft, then push the key into it, smooth it over a bit and rewrap it and put it back in the fridge to get hard. No one would ever find it."

I laughed. "You should be a jewel thief."

"I probably should," she said, sounding serious. "I bet I'd be a great thief."

Chapter Six

Thursday, 12:17 PM, HST

True to her word, Buttaree showed up at my place almost every night during the next week or so, bringing food from various Honolulu establishments that were still open at that time of night. We sat around eating, drinking beer, smoking weed, and talking story, as we say here in Hawaii. We really got along exceptionally well, which was a little odd, considering our different backgrounds. But I enjoyed her company and she seemed to like spending time with me.

On my part, that was probably because deep down where I didn't want to deal with it, I had the hots for her and was hoping our friendship would turn into a physical relationship. You know – sex. And the reason I didn't want to deal with those feelings was because I knew that in a short time Buttaree would be moving along to another gig somewhere, and ours was a relationship that was destined to be short-term. I wasn't sure how I'd react to her leaving if we ended up in a boyfriend-girlfriend situation.

There was some guilt involved, too. About wanting a sexual relationship with her, I mean. Of course, a guy wanting to have sex with a good-looking girl isn't unusual, but Buttaree and I were friends now and I felt like I might be taking advantage of her if I pushed for a more-physical relationship.

And there was something else, as well. Deep down – deep, deep, way down – I knew there was another motivation behind my desire to convert our friendship into a romance. And it was for the shallowest, basest of reasons – so that, at some point in the future I could say,

"Yeah, I had a stripper girlfriend once upon a time," and it would be true. Like I said – shallow. I felt ashamed just knowing that thought had crossed my mind.

So, there was all that. But, if I were really being truthful with myself, the reason I did little beyond hope that we'd end up in bed was because I was afraid I'd screw things up by trying to add romance to the equation. I'd become convinced that our friendship depended almost entirely on the fact I hadn't hit on her – that she enjoyed being with a guy who wasn't constantly trying to get in her pants. And so I did nothing.

Other than the fact that I treated her as a friend instead of a sex object, I have no idea what Buttaree saw in me. I'm just an average-looking guy. There's nothing special about me at all. In fact, I once overheard a girl describe me as, "that slacker haole guy who always needs a haircut." And, although my feelings were hurt at the time, that actually was a pretty good description of who I was and who I am. Except for that part about me being a haole – I'm *hapa*, a Hawaiian word used to describe locals of mixed race, like me and Kimo.

Sometimes I wondered if Buttaree thought I was gay, even though I'd indicated to her on more than one occasion that I liked girls. Perhaps she thought the reason I hadn't made a play for her – if she wondered about it at all – was because I wasn't interested in her in that way. Maybe I should bring up the subject again and remind her that I'm a typical heterosexual male, a little on the shy side around girls but otherwise 100% normal when it comes to that boy-girl thing.

The more I thought about it, the more that seemed like a good idea. To talk to her about my burgeoning feelings toward her, I mean. Just hint at them – maybe say something like, "I think I'm developing a crush on you," then laugh, as if it was a joke, and see what kind of a reaction I got.

So when I bumped into her in the hallway on Thursday around noon, I decided it was time for us to have "the talk" – time for me to tell her about my feelings toward her. Or at least hint at them.

"You coming over tonight?" I said.

"Absolutely."

"Really?" Her answer was a little surprising. Most of the time, if I asked, Buttaree committed to our late-night meetings with a "Maybe," or a "Probably."

"Yeah. I've been thinking. You and I need to have a talk. A serious talk," she said.

Well, this wasn't turning out the way I'd expected. She'd stolen my carefully-considered plan to have a serious talk with her. "About what?" I said.

"There's some stuff I need to tell you, that's all. I've been thinking about it for a while and I finally decided, so ... see you tonight, then, and I'll lay it all out for you. Okay?"

"Yeah, sure."

"Toodles," she said with a smile, and walked off down the hall.

I watched as she got on the elevator, gave her a little wave goodbye, then went inside my apartment, got a beer from the fridge and settled into my favorite spot on the couch. Once again, I had some serious thinking to do.

First off, what the hell was going on? It was like we'd reversed roles. I'd been planning to say the same things to her that she'd said to me – that I'd been thinking about it for a while and decided we needed to have a serious talk. Was it possible we both wanted to talk about the same subject? Could it be that Buttaree had developed a soft spot in her heart for little old me? I mentally crossed my fingers and made a wish, at the same time remembering that old adage, 'Be careful what you wish for, lest it come true.'

Evidently, while I was considering all this, I nodded off, because the next thing I knew I was looking at my clock and it was almost two. I got up, splashed some water on my face, changed into my bathing suit and headed out the door, intending to go to the beach.

Kuhio Beach – that's the real name of the beach most folks call Waikiki Beach – is a three-minute walk from my apartment. Just go straight down Paoakalani until you come to Kalakaua Avenue and there's the world-famous beach, right across the street. I usually hit it up three or four afternoons a week for an hour or so, just to work on my tan and to check out the wide array of bikinis on exhibit.

That's where I was headed when I saw the guy Buttaree claimed was stalking her. At least, I thought it was him. He was sitting on the bus bench on Kuhio Avenue as I waited for the light to change, looking exactly as she'd described him – an old, gray-haired haole guy with a big, bushy mustache, wearing shorts, a blue aloha shirt and a blue baseball cap. It had to be him. I made a quick decision to go talk to him but before I could cross the street and approach him, he hopped aboard an oncoming bus and disappeared down Kuhio, heading into the heart of Waikiki.

So perhaps Buttaree wasn't paranoid, I decided as I crossed Kuhio and continued on my way to the beach. That guy could be stalking her. Or maybe he was just a local guy who lived around here and who also liked to frequent strip clubs. Whichever it was, I'd be keeping an eye out for him in the future, and if I saw him again, I'd make sure to ask him about it.

Chapter Seven

Friday, 2:14 AM, HST

A particularly slow night at work led to the entire packing crew – me and six others – being sent home early. I took a quick shower, straightened up the living room a bit, then grabbed a beer and settled onto my couch to wait for Buttaree to come home from work. While I waited, I mentally rehearsed what I wanted to say to her.

What I was looking for was a way to ease into the conversation, a plan that would let me find out how she felt about me without me having to reveal too much about my feelings for her. I know – that's a really cowardly approach. But I was afraid I might blurt out something like, "I think I'm falling for you, Buttaree," only to have her tell me she didn't think of me in "that way." And that would be the end of our friendship.

Of course, I might not have to say anything at all. After all, she'd said she wanted to have a 'serious' talk with me. Maybe all I'd have to do was listen and she'd be the one to say, "I think I'm falling for you." The thought brought a smile to my face ... and then a frown. If only life was really that easy.

I lit up a joint, took a big hit and held it until I started to cough. Easing my lung's and throat's discomfort with a long swallow of beer, I hit the joint again, more gently this time. The big blue numbers on my digital clock, sitting across the room next to the TV, told me it was a quarter to three. Buttaree should be tapping on my door any minute now.

Fifteen minutes went by. Three o'clock and she still hadn't shown up. I got another beer and finished the last of the joint. A nice buzz had taken hold of my brain but, as sometimes happens when I smoke weed, the pleasant sensations were accompanied by a slight amount of paranoia. It wasn't like Buttaree to be this late, and I began to worry.

What if she'd been right when she thought those guys at the club were planning to kidnap her? She could be, right now, tied up in the trunk of a car, headed to the airport where a private plane was waiting to whisk her off to some foreign country, where she'd be sold to some gazillionaire for big bucks! Or ... maybe she was just delayed at work. With only those two possibilities stuck in my head, I started to become really worried. So I texted her.

When five minutes went by without a reply, I called her. No answer there, either. That was unusual – the only time I'd ever seen Buttaree without her phone was that first night when she'd showed up, naked, at my apartment. The thought occurred to me that perhaps she'd forgotten about our planned get-together and was already home. Maybe in the shower, where she couldn't hear her phone. I struggled to my feet and headed over to her apartment, intending to see if that was the case.

An odd thing happened when I knocked on her door. It swung open. Not a lot, just three or four inches, but it was enough to reveal that the lights were on. In addition, the sound of running water from the bathroom drifted out into the hallway, so I knew she was home. I knocked more loudly on the door and called, "Hey, Buttaree!" but I guess she couldn't hear me over the sound of the water.

I pushed open the door and went in. Buttaree's bathroom was similarly situated as the one in my apartment – on the right, down a short hallway, with a door into the hallway and another into her bedroom. I knocked on the hallway door. "Buttaree?"

No answer.

Using considerably more force, I knocked again. Loudly.

Nothing. Very strange.

I cracked open the door and peeked inside, expecting to be greeted by a barrage of steam, but there was none. Only a slight rush of moistness greeted me as I stuck my head into the room. "Buttaree? You in here?" I said. A bad feeling began a slow climb up my spine as I swung open the door and stepped into the bathroom.

It wasn't the shower I'd heard running. It was water running into an almost-full tub and then out the overflow drain. I went over to turn it off and that's when I saw her. She was in the tub, dressed in her usual outfit of shorts and halter top, staring up at me with open eyes from a couple of inches under the water. Although I had no medical training and had never seen a dead person up close before, I was pretty sure that Buttaree was dead.

I leaned over the tub and turned off the water, thinking that people who accidentally drown in the tub are usually not wearing clothes, so this was probably not an accident. It was when I stood back up that it hit me. Not figuratively. Literally. Something – no, someone – hit me in the back of the head with an object I would later describe to the police as "very, very hard." As I crumpled to the floor with only a vague idea of what was happening, darkness rushed in at me from multiple directions.

I wasn't unconscious for long, but when I woke up I immediately regretted it – my head hurt like hell and my stomach felt like I'd eaten too much of my Aunt Limulani's extra-hot, Hawaiian-style chili. A quick glance at the tub reminded me of what had recently occurred here and brought forth an almost-instantaneous, panicked rush of intestinal juices from my gut. In other words, I puked. I leaned over the toilet and barfed – long and loud.

In addition to throbbing pain, my head also held a lot of confusion. Whether that was from the blow I'd suffered or from the situation I now found myself in, I wasn't sure. But, never having found a dead body before, I didn't quite know what to do next.

Checking out the rest of Buttaree's apartment seemed like a logical next step, so I did that. But an extremely cautious inspection tour revealed it to be empty. Whoever had conked me on the head was gone, having left the front door wide open in what I assumed was a haste to depart. I returned to the bathroom.

Buttaree was still in the tub. And still dead. It was strange. As I looked down at her lifeless body, the main emotion I was feeling was not one of sorrow at having lost a friend and potential romantic partner, but of shock at finding myself in this predicament. Discovering a dead body, I mean.

After forcing my muddled brain to think about things for a while, I decided there was nothing I could do about what had happened here and the obvious next step was to call the police. After all, murders were their domain, and this was obviously a murder. I headed back to my apartment, where I'd left my phone.

As I left and closed the door, I noticed the lock was broken and there was a little bit of broken wood around it. I hadn't spotted that earlier when I first came over here. Obviously, someone had forced it open. I didn't know for sure who that someone was, but there was one person who was high on my list of suspects – the old guy with the bushy mustache and blue aloha shirt that I'd seen earlier, when I was on my way to the beach.

Chapter Eight

Friday, 6:08 AM HST

Cops were everywhere. In Buttaree's apartment, in my apartment, they bustled about, examining things and tapping notes into tablets. I worried they might check out my ashtray – the one with a half-dozen roaches in it – but they ignored it. A tired-looking HPD homicide investigator and I sat at my kitchen table, discussing the events that led to my discovering Buttaree's body. I'd already spent more than 10 minutes giving him personal information, and now he was asking about our relationship.

"So you two were supposed to hook up after work?" said Detective Higa, the investigator. He was at least 60 years old, of Okinawan descent, judging from his name, his slight stature, and his leathery, heavily-wrinkled, dark bronze skin. Although technically Japanese, Okinawans are ethnically different and have the ability to tan to a deep, golden bronze, while true Japanese burn to a nice, crispy red – which is what happens to me if I'm not careful. Plus, Higa is an Okinawan name, not Japanese.

"Not hook up. She was going to come over, have a couple of beers with me and shoot the shit. We were friends, that's all. We did that frequently."

"That's what I meant by hook up," he said, looking slightly puzzled

"Whatevahs." I guess I should have known his definition and mine would be different.

"How frequently?" Detective Higa said. "How often did the two of you ... uh, get together?"

"Oh, I don't know. Maybe three or four times a week. I just met her a couple of weeks ago, so this was kind of a new thing."

"How did that happen? How did you meet her?"

"Well, she lives right across the hall ..."

"So? What? You bumped into each other in the hall and started talking, something like that?"

"Not exactly." I told him the story of how Buttaree had shown up at my door a couple of weeks earlier, worried someone was in her apartment. I left out the part about her being naked.

"Do you know if she filed a report?"

"Actually, I called 911 and they sent a couple of officers over to check out the place. But they didn't find anything. No one was there."

"I don't suppose you remember the names of the officers, do you?"

"Yeah. I do. One was a haole guy named Jenkins and the other officer's name was Cabacungan. He looked Japanese, though, not Filipino. I think they were from that group of officers who patrol Waikiki on bicycles."

"Short pants?"

"Yeah."

Detective Higa nodded and wrote the names down in a tiny notebook – the paper kind, not some mini-tablet or computer. "And so tonight, she was supposed to come over, and when she didn't, you went looking for her. Right?"

"That's right."

"And you discovered her in the tub? Dead?"

"Unfortunately, yes."

"I'm sorry for your loss. Were you close friends?"

"Well, like I said, I only met her recently. But we were getting along pretty well so, yeah, I guess you could say we were pretty close friends. Or on the way to becoming close, anyway."

"I see."

"I think maybe I was developing a crush on her," I said, and then immediately regretted saying it. *Haven't you ever seen a detective movie?* piped up that little voice inside my head. *Never, ever, EVER volunteer information!*

"You don't say?" Detective Higa scribbled something – most likely what I just told him – into his notebook. "Is that why the two of you were getting together tonight? So you could tell her about these feelings for her?"

"Not really. It was like I said earlier. She was gonna come over, we'd have a couple of beers and talk story. That's all."

"And the feelings?"

"I was ... just taking it slow. I liked her, you know, but I didn't want to scare her away by bringing it up too early, so I was ... just ..."

"Taking it slow," he said, finishing my train of thought.

"Yeah."

"Did you kill her, Archie?" He leaned forward and looked intently at my face. "Was it you who killed Buttaree Gudnis?"

Shocked, I jumped back, slamming into the back of my chair. "What! Are you nuts? Why would I kill her? She was my friend!"

"I know, but sometimes these lovers' quarrels –"

"We weren't lovers!" I practically yelled at him. "And there was no quarrel. Stop making things up!"

"All right, all right. Calm down. These are questions I have to ask," Detective Higa said. "So what happened after you discovered the body?"

I took a deep breath and exhaled. "I got conked on the head with something very, very hard."

"I see," he said, again scribbling in his notebook. "How, exactly, did that go down? Describe it for me."

"Well, the water in the tub was running, so I leaned down and turned it off. And when I straightened back up, he hit me in the back of the head." I leaned forward and showed him the rather large bump that had appeared where I'd been hit.

"You should get that looked at," he said.

"Yeah, I will."

"So then what happened? After you got hit."

"I blacked out."

"For how long?"

"I'm not sure, exactly. Not long, judging by the time when I got back here and called you guys. About 10 minutes, maybe a little less."

"I see. You said when you turned the water off, he hit you on the back of the head. Right?"

"When I stood back up, yeah."

"Did you see him? Or anybody?"

"No."

"You said 'he' hit you. Why do you think it was a man?"

"I'm just assuming," I said.

"Could it have been a woman?"

"I guess so."

Detective Higa paused for a few seconds to make another entry in his notebook, then said, "Do you know of anyone who might want to hurt Miss Gudnis? Anyone who was mad at her, who held a grudge, anything like that?"

"No. But ..."

"But what?"

"Well, she said she thought she had a stalker."

"Really?"

"Yeah, she said she kept seeing this guy. At work, down where she used to live, even down here on Kuhio Avenue. I thought maybe she was just being overly dramatic, or paranoid, but then I saw him. Right down here on the corner, getting on the bus." I pointed toward the corner of Kuhio and Paoakalani.

"You saw her stalker?"

"Yeah. At least, I think it was him."

"So you know what he looks like?"

"Yeah. She told me."

"So tell me," he said.

I described Buttaree's stalker, or fan, or whatever he was – maybe just a neighbor – in detail for Detective Higa, being careful to recount every sighting she'd told me about, including the time he came to the club with a couple of 'hoods' she thought might be going to kidnap her. He wrote it all down.

"Let me see if I've got this straight. Old haole guy, bushy gray mustache, dirty white shorts, blue aloha shirt and a blue baseball cap. That about right?"

"And slippahs. And he had a pretty good tan, too, so he was probably local."

Detective Higa gave me a strange look and added the information into his little book.

"You know him?" I asked. "You know somebody who looks like that?"

He didn't answer, instead closing his notebook and getting to his feet. "I think that's it for now," he said. "If I have any more questions, I'll be in touch."

"Okay." I stood up and walked with him to my front door. "So, is that it?"

"It?"

"Yeah. Are you finished with me? With all these questions and stuff?"

"For now. I may have more questions later, as the case develops. If I do, I'll be in touch." He turned and shook my hand. "Thank you for your cooperation, Mr. Morris."

"It's Archie," I said.

"Archie. All right." For the first time since I'd met him, he smiled. "Let me give you a piece of advice, Archie."

"All right," I replied, even though his remark hadn't been a question.

"Don't go anywhere."

"What?"

"Don't go anywhere," he said. "Don't be taking a trip to the neighbor islands, or the mainland, or anywhere, for a while. Stay home."

"Am I a suspect?

"No. We don't have any suspects – yet. And until we do, just about everyone on the island is a person of interest. You, my friend, are our number one person of interest right now, since it was you who discovered the body." He tapped me lightly on the chest with one finger. "So stay home. Taking a trip at this stage of the investigation would look really suspicious."

"That's just great," I said, even though I didn't have any trips planned for the near future. It seemed odd that a cop would be advising me on how to appear innocent. I wondered if this was some police trick, meant to throw suspects off their guard.

"I wouldn't worry too much about it if you're really innocent –"

"I am!" I said.

"Well, let's hope so." He turned and started to leave, then turned back. "Like I said, don't worry too much about it. I've already checked you out a bit – I know you don't have a criminal record, for example. That's always a good start." He gave me a little wave of his hand and left, heading toward Buttaree's apartment, where several uniformed officers were standing around her front door, apparently doing nothing.

I closed the door and stood there in a slight state of shock. Not only was Buttaree dead, evidently I was the chief – maybe the only – suspect, even though I was being called 'a person of interest.' And on top of that disturbing piece of news, I had a headache that, on a scale of one to ten, would have been a twelve. Getting whacked on the head will do that to you, I guess.

Detective Higa had mentioned I should get my head checked out, and while that sounded like a good idea, it meant a trip over to the Princess Kaiulani Hotel, where there was a walk-in clinic. Although the clinic was intended mainly for tourists, I used it almost exclusively for my healthcare. The problem was parking. There wasn't any, and it was a fairly long walk from my apartment over to the hotel and back, especially for someone who'd been hit on the head and might have a concussion. So that meant a taxi, and waiting for it to show up, and another taxi to bring me home, and ... do you see where I'm going with this?

On the other hand, my bedroom was only a room away, and I had the feeling that what I really needed was not a trip to a clinic but a good night's sleep. Or actually, since the sun was already up, a good day's sleep.

I popped a couple of aspirins and climbed into bed, opting for sleep over doctors. As I lay there, waiting for the arms of Morpheus to overtake me, I pondered recent events. It was strange, I thought, that all of Detective Higa's questions had been about me. He hadn't asked me hardly anything about Buttaree. You'd think, since I was one of her few acquaintances here in Honolulu, that I'd be a major source of information about her. Perhaps another detective was handling that part of the investigation, I decided. I wondered where he was getting his information, what with Buttaree being dead and everything.

The memory of Buttaree lying face up in the tub came flooding back into my brain. What a way to die. A couple of tears trickled down my cheek as I realized I'd never see her again. Poor Buttaree.

And poor me, too. This wasn't what I signed up for. I was completely innocent and yet now I was the number one suspect in a murder!

I rolled over and covered my head with my pillow. There were plenty of questions floating through my head – who killed Buttaree and why, for example – but as I nodded off, only one question really seemed to matter. What the hell had I gotten myself into?

Chapter Nine

Friday

It was a restless sleep, obviously made that way by the previous night's hellish event. I woke frequently and my time spent asleep was filled with strange, confusing dreams about Buttaree, me, and Detective Higa. Remembering dreams has never been a strong point with me, but in one of them, at least, it seemed the three of us were having a picnic in nearby Kapiolani Park.

Hunger finally forced me out of bed about three in the afternoon. It had been almost 24 hours since I'd had anything to eat – I'd been expecting Buttaree to bring something the night before. There was also that little barfing incident that took place after I regained consciousness. The combination of those events had left me with an empty, angry stomach that grumbled and groaned, demanding food. I took a quick shower and headed out, intending to grab a couple of burgers over on Kapahulu Avenue, about a five-minute walk away.

As I left, I noticed the door to Buttaree's place was covered with crime-scene tape, ostensibly as a warning to those with bad intentions. More like an invitation, was my opinion. *Hey! Look! This place is empty. Come on in and take a look around – see what you can find!* Not wanting to be reminded of what happened in that apartment the night before, I tried to avoid looking at it as I made my way down the hall to the elevator.

I was back home in less than 20 minutes, comfortably parked on my couch, chowing down on burgers, fries, and onion rings, with a nice cold beer to wash it all down, when my phone rang. It was Kimo.

"Yeah. What's up?" I mumbled through a mouthful of food.

"Hey, howzit? You all right?"

"Yeah. Why?"

"You sound funny."

"I'm eating."

"Oh. You want me to call back?"

"No, I'm good."

"I heard about what happened. With your friend, Buttaree."

"Yeah? How'd you hear about that so soon? Was it on the news?"

"I don't think so – not yet. Pops told me about it."

Pops was Kimo's dad, who always had better information than the local TV stations, anyway, since he spent most days hanging around the police station, talking story with his old buddies. He claimed it was so he could recruit employees for his business, but everyone in the family – and me, too – knew it was because he just couldn't get being a cop out of his system. "What did he tell you?" I said.

"Not that much. Just that someone killed Buttaree – drowned her in the tub. That's nasty, killing her that way."

"Yeah," I agreed. Drowning was a nasty way of murdering a person.

"So how's your head? I heard you got whacked."

"It's okay. There's a lump where he hit me. But it doesn't hurt that much anymore."

"Pops said you're a suspect."

"I figured that, since I found the body."

"Actually, he said you're the only suspect. At least, for now."

"I'm not surprised," I said, popping the last of the onion rings into my mouth. "Anything else?"

"Not really. They took Buttaree's body to the morgue. I guess they're going to do an autopsy."

"I think they do that for any unattended death." I finished my second burger and the last of the fries at exactly the same time, feeling pretty proud of my pacing prowess as I rewarded myself with a large swallow of beer.

"Yeah, I think so," he said. "Hey, listen, about tomorrow –"

"What? You can't make it?"

"Yeah."

"What's her name this time?"

He laughed. "I nevah can fool you. I was gonna tell you I had to work. It's Kelly."

"What happened to whatsername? Donna?"

"Nothing. She's still around. We're getting together next Wednesday. But Kelly's taking me up to Makaha for the weekend. Two days and nights in a luxury suite, her treat."

It was my turn to laugh. "You're terrible," I said.

"I told you before, I'm a playah."

"I never doubted it."

"So, listen, you sure you're okay? You're not, like, all depressed and stuff, are you? I know you were gonna make a play for her – Buttaree."

"I'm fine," I said, which was only partially true. "Just bummed out, not depressed."

"Okay. I was thinking, you gonna take some time off from work? To recover?"

"Yeah. Maybe a few days. I think I got a concussion. I'm gonna call my boss on Monday and tell him what happened."

"Then, how's about I come over on Monday? After work. We can sit around, have a few beers, maybe even take a walk down to Kalakaua and see what's going on. Oh, and I'll tell you about my weekend with Kelly. Did I mention she's super-hot?"

"No, but I figured she was. You better hope Donna doesn't find out – she'll stop giving you weed."

"Yeah," he said, laughing. "It's a dangerous game, being a playah."

"I wouldn't know," I said.

"So, about Monday?"

"Yeah, Monday's fine. Bring beer."

"I always bring beer, bruddah. Haven't you noticed?"

"Sure. I haven't had to buy beer in years. Or weed, either. You're the best friend ... *evah!*"

"You, too," he said, laughing. "See ya Monday. About five or so."

"Laters, then."

"Laters," he said, and hung up.

I traded in my used beer for a new model, lit up a joint and leaned back to think about how my life had turned to crap. It wasn't just the murder of Buttaree and me being a suspect – I was a 27-year-old college dropout with a lousy job, a hopeless future, and not much idea of what to do with my life. I strongly suspected my mom was right when she said inheriting all that money and this apartment was the worst thing that ever happened to me.

Still, life goes on, as they say. And there's a stupid expression, if I ever heard one. Life goes on. Duh! Of course. It either goes on or it stops, and there's not much you can do about it. That's just the way things work.

I was still sitting on the couch, feeling sorry for myself, when my doorbell rang at about five o'clock. Since I wasn't expecting company, the thought that the police were paying me a return visit immediately popped into my head. Great! Just what me and an apartment filled with marijuana smoke needed – a visit from the police. I padded quietly to the door.

My peephole revealed three people standing in the hall – two men and a woman. But they weren't cops. I recognized the woman as a reporter from channel 9 news and one of the men was holding a medium-size TV camera. Apparently they were here to make me famous on the local news. Or perhaps, since I was the chief suspect in a particularly-unpleasant murder, their intention was to make me infamous.

I returned to the couch, making as little noise as possible. The doorbell rang again. I ignored it. It rang again, followed by several loud knocks. I paid no attention to any of it and eventually they gave up and went away, presumably because they thought I wasn't home.

A glimpse of what my life might be like in the immediate future floated into my head, and it wasn't a pretty picture. Reporters were hounding me, the police were giving interviews implying that I was the only one who could possibly have murdered Buttaree, and the headline in the Star-Advertiser read, *Stripper Murdered: Local Schmuck Suspected.* And, of course, that local schmuck was me!

Chapter Ten

Monday

    I spent the entire weekend in a funk, sad about Buttaree's demise and worried about my own involvement in the matter. When I wasn't in bed, I sprawled on my couch, lost in a fog of marijuana smoke, beer buzz, and self-pity. I turned off my phone. The occasional chiming of my doorbell and knocks on the door went unanswered. Reporters, probably. Or maybe the cops. Either way, I wasn't in the mood to be interviewed.

Scientists claim a blow to the head can sometimes produce curious side effects. People have reported that, after being struck in the head, they could suddenly speak a foreign language, or solve complicated math problems, or even understand Shakespeare! Maybe something like that was what was happening with me, because I'm not normally the kind of person who sits around, moping, trying to comprehend the meaning of life and where I fit into things. Perhaps my entire 'down-in-the-dumps' weekend was caused by getting whacked in the head. And, of course, Buttaree getting murdered.

Anyway, by the time Kimo showed up at about five-thirty Monday afternoon, pounding on my door and yelling, "Hey, Archie! Open up!" I was more than ready to climb out of the hole I'd been in and put my misery behind me.

"Whoa! You look like crap, bruddah!" he said when I opened the door.

"Nice to see you, too." I took the proffered 12-pack and bag of assorted goodies from him and headed toward the kitchen.

"Bring me a beer when you come back," he called.

I stored the beer away in my fridge, grabbed two frosty bottles from my own stash and returned with them to the living room, where Kimo had made himself comfortable on the couch. I handed him a beer and joined him.

"So, you okay?" he said, taking a long pull on his beer.

"Yeah, I'll live. Unless I'm lucky."

He ignored my negativity. "Did you know there's like a hundred reporters hanging around downstairs? Outside."

"A hundred?"

"Well, more like three or four, probably. They asked me if I knew you."

"I'll bet that was a mistake on their part. What did you tell them?"

"I asked them to repeat your name," he said, chuckling. "And I told them I knew an Archie once, but his last name was Williams, not Morris. Also, his family moved back to the mainland when I was about 12 years old, so it most likely wasn't him – you, I mean. And then I started telling them about how this Archie Williams guy was real tall – even taller than I was back then – and how I bet he grew up to be a really good basketball player. And finally, I volunteered to be interviewed on camera, telling them I'd say whatever they wanted me to."

"What happened?" I said, managing to come up with a laugh in spite of my melancholy.

"They just, sort of ... started backing away from me. Like I was *lolo*."

"You *are* crazy, man."

"But in a good way, right?"

"Yeah. In a good way." I lit a joint and passed it over. "So how was your weekend with Kelly?"

A sour look descended over his face. "Don't even ask," he said, taking a hit.

"Okay. Forget I mentioned it."

"It was a disaster, a complete disaster," he said, and started to tell me about it. "It wasn't just the two of us. There was another couple, too."

"Yeah?"

"Yeah."

"Who?"

"Her parents."

I started laughing. "Really? Her parents?"

"Uh-huh. The other couple was Carl and Jennifer, Kelly's parents. Nice people, actually."

The laughs continued – on my part, not so much Kimo's. "So what did you do all weekend?"

"Well, lots of things, but I didn't get to do what I really wanted to."

"Which was – ?"

"Kelly, of course. I wanted to do Kelly."

I laughed some more. "Tough luck."

"There'll be another time, I'm sure," he said, his face brightening.

Being around Kimo usually puts me in a better mood. He's one of those people who almost always exudes positive energy and elevates the spirits of those around him. I say 'almost' because he's also not a guy you want to cross – because of his size and all-around athletic ability, he's more than able to throttle back that positivity and bring forth his negative side. Which is my way of saying, you'd want him on your side in a fight.

We sat in silence for a while, smoking and drinking. Eventually Kimo said, "Did you eat?"

"This morning."

"I'm starving."

"Me, too," I said. "It's the weed."

"Whatevahs. I'm hungry."

"So let's go get something to eat."

"Yeah, that sounds good. What about those guys out front? The reporters."

"We can go out the back," I said. "There's a little alley next to that apartment building behind us. It comes out on Ohua Avenue."

"Great. Go get ready. You can't go out looking like that!" He made a face and pointed at me, then laughed.

I spent a couple of minutes washing up, combing my hair, and trying to make myself look like I hadn't just escaped from prison by digging a tunnel. Changing my clothes helped a lot but, since I hadn't shaved recently, there wasn't much I could do about my four-day-old growth of beard. Not that it really mattered – stubble was currently in style.

"Let's go," I said, when I'd done all I could to turn myself into a presentable person.

"Not much of an improvement," Kimo noted, grinning.

I grabbed my keys and we headed out. As I was locking up, a noise – a slight thud, like a book dropping on a floor – called my attention to Buttaree's apartment. Something wasn't right over there. The crime-scene tape had been pulled down and was piled haphazardly next to the door, which was slightly ajar, revealing that lights were on inside the apartment. "Look," I said to Kimo, and pointed across the hall.

"I am looking," he said. "That tape was up when I arrived – I noticed it."

"Wonder what's going on."

"It's probably the cops. Or maybe some of those reporters."

"Kinda strange, though," I said.

"What?"

I glanced at my watch. "It's almost seven. Seems like an odd time for cops to be ... to be ... well, I don't know what they'd be doing in there at this time of night – I thought they were finished with her apartment. They spent hours in there the other night, collecting clues and stuff, plus they put up that crime-scene tape. That usually means they're finished, doesn't it?"

"Then maybe it's a reporter."

"Yeah. Maybe."

"Let's go check it out," he said. "It could even be the murderer, come back to ... " His voice trailed off.

"To do what?"

"I dunno. Whatever it is that murderers do, I guess." He paused for a second, looking thoughtful. "Did you ever ask yourself why Buttaree got murdered?"

"I've thought about it, yeah. But without knowing who did it, it's impossible to figure out why."

"So maybe it wasn't a murder, at all. Maybe it was an accident."

"An accident? Buttaree's murder? How is drowning someone in a tub an accident?"

"I've been thinking about it and I've got a theory. Whoever killed her was looking for something and Buttaree knew where it was but she wouldn't tell him, so he put her in the tub and was, kinda, like, torturing her by dunking her under the water in order to get her to talk. And when she wouldn't tell him, he drowned her. Accidentally."

I looked at him, impressed. "That's actually a terrific theory. It makes a lot of sense. Who knew you were so smart?"

"Gotta confess. It's not really my theory. I got it from Pops."

"Yeah?"

"He said it's something the cops were considering."

"That's terrific news. I wish you'd told me that earlier."

"Well ... it was good news. But they dismissed it."

"What! But it makes perfect sense."

"I thought so, too. But they like you for the murder." He grinned and punched me in the arm. Lightly, fortunately.

I lowered my voice, pointed at Buttareee's place, and said conspiratorially, "You know, he could be in there, right now. The murderer. Searching for whatever it was that Buttaree wouldn't tell him about."

"Or couldn't tell him because she didn't know. But –"

"But what?"

"Didn't the police already search the place?"

"Yeah, but they didn't find anything. At least, not that I've heard about."

"So let's go take a look. Maybe we'll catch us a killer and you'll go from being a suspect to a hero."

"All right. Let's do it," I said, feeling extra-brave with my extra-large friend by my side.

Chapter Eleven

With me right behind him, Kimo pushed open the door to Buttaree's apartment and peeked inside.

"See anything?" I whispered.

"Shh," he whispered back, turning his head and putting a finger to his mouth. "Someone's in the kitchen – that's where the light's coming from."

We went inside, closing the door behind us and making our way cautiously down the short hallway toward the kitchen. When we got to the doorway, we saw the cause of the discarded crime-scene tape, the light, and the noise I'd heard. And it wasn't the police. Or a reporter, either. The intruder was the old guy with the blue aloha shirt and blue baseball cap – Buttaree's former stalker.

He was kneeling on the floor, his back to us, pulling out stuff from under the sink, completely unaware of our presence. We watched as he removed each bottle or can of what looked like cleaning products, examined it briefly, then set it aside.

"Looking for something?" Kimo said to him.

I don't think I've ever seen anyone, especially an older person, move as fast as he did when he heard Kimo's voice. He leapt to his feet and spun around at the same time, landing in a sort-of karate pose, apparently intended to show he was ready to fight. However, he wasn't a very big guy and when Kimo took two steps toward him, his eyes widened and he appeared to recognize the seriousness of his situation – him, about five feet ten and 150 pounds, and Kimo, about six-seven and over 300 pounds. His demeanor changed. He dropped his hands to his side, smiled and said, "Hey, bruddah. Howzit?"

Kimo wasn't buying the friendly local routine. "What are you doing in here?" he said, his voice decidedly unfriendly.

"Well, ... uh, ..." His eyes darted wildly around the room, apparently searching for an escape route as he stalled for time. Unfortunately for him, the only way out of the apartment was down the hallway, right past Kimo. And me, too, of course.

"I asked you a question," Kimo said. His voice was calm, but with undertones of, if I don't get an answer voluntarily, I'll just beat it out of you.

The old guy's skittering eyes left the kitchen and began a search of the open dining room and living room area, eventually landing on the glass doors leading to the lanai and seeming to stick there. Perhaps he thought that was his way out.

"Thinking of jumping?" said Kimo. "We're on the fifth floor. It must be about 50 feet down to the ground, but go ahead if you want to – I won't stop you. In fact, I'll even help you, if you want." He took another step forward.

"No, no. That's not what I want."

"Then answer the question. What are you doing here?"

"I'm ... uh, conducting a search."

"Really? What are you searching for?"

"Well, that's the funny thing, ya know. I don't really know the answer to that."

"That sounds ... unbelievable," Kimo said.

"It's true. My name is Thomas Mangrum," he said, sticking out his hand in a proffered handshake. Kimo ignored it.

"I'm a private investigator," he continued. "I was hired to search this place and see if I could find anything interesting, that's all."

"Hired? By who?"

"I can't tell you that."

"Oh, that's disappointing. Professional ethics, is that it?

"Yeah, it's confidential."

"You got a badge? A license? Something like that?"

"No."

"Business card?"

"I, uh ... tend not to carry those kinds of items when I'm, like, you know, working."

"Oh, yeah. I get it. Well, okay. I guess we're not going to get any information out of you, then." Kimo laughed and stuck out his hand.

What?!! What the hell was Kimo thinking, letting this guy go? I had tons of questions I wanted to ask him. Like, why he was following Buttaree, for example. And who were the two guys with him that night, watching Buttaree at Busteroo's?

Distracted by my displeasure over Kimo's words, I didn't see exactly what happened next. One second he and Thomas Mangrum were about to shake hands and the next second Kimo had grabbed the old guy by his middle finger and bent it back so far that Mangrum was dancing and yelping in pain.

"So, you were saying? About who hired you?" Kimo said.

The old guy was a pretty good dancer – for his age. He also provided some spontaneous but overly-repetitive rap lyrics to accompany his gyrations. They went, "I can't tell you! I can't tell you! I can't tell you!" As I said – overly repetitive.

Kimo, however, seemed less than impressed with Mangrum's dancing and rapping abilities. He applied a little more pressure to the finger, causing the old guy to move into ballet mode – up on his toes. His rap stayed the same, though – 'I can't tell you.'

Evidently the fingers of older people do not bend as easily as those of younger ones. Or perhaps Kimo just underestimated his own strength, because it was at about this time that Thomas Mangrum's song and dance routine came to a sudden conclusion, punctuated by a loud snapping sound. He opened his mouth to scream but no sound came out. Instead, his eyes rolled up into his head and he collapsed, straight down, like a marionette with cut strings.

"Shit, Kimo! You killed him!" I said, looking down at the limp body on Buttaree's kitchen floor.

He laughed. "He ain't dead. He fainted. Get a glass of water."

I got some water from the sink and handed it to him. He poured a little into the cupped palm of his left hand and, using the fingers of his right hand, splashed some of it into Mangrum's face. Nothing happened. He smiled up at me and said, "Maybe you were right. Maybe he is dead!"

He took the remainder of the water and dumped about half of it directly onto the old guy's face. Coughing and spitting, Mangrum sputtered back to life, evidently not dead at all.

"Hey, welcome back, bruddah," Kimo said.

Mangrum looked down at his hand, where his finger was growing fatter and darker by the minute, then up at Kimo. "What the hell is wrong with you, man? You broke my finger!"

"Yeah, I did. One down, nine to go." Kimo grinned, dragged Mangrum to his feet and plunked him down onto a kitchen chair. "Now, I believe you were about to tell me who hired you," he said.

Chapter Twelve

"Okay, okay," Thomas Mangrum said. "I'll talk. Just leave my fingers alone. This hurts like hell, you know. I don't suppose you have any aspirin, do you?"

"No. So talk," Kimo said.

I stood to one side, watching all this. Kimo's ability to take charge of this situation was impressive, although I wasn't surprised. I'd seen him in a couple of fights and he always managed to put a swift end to them – his opponents invariably seemed shocked at how quickly a man his size could move. And also, how hard he could punch!

"Well, a couple of weeks ago, I get a call from this guy in California – Richard Harrodi, that's his name. But he goes by Harry. 'Call me Harry,' he says. Anyway, he wants me to find this chick, this Buttaree Gudnis, and when I find her, keep an eye on her. He sends a grand to my PayPal account and promises me another grand later on. So, I figure, with a name like that, she had to be a stripper, ya know, so –"

"That's her real name," I said, interrupting.

He looked over at me, apparently realizing for the first time that I was there. "Howzit?" he said.

I nodded back at him.

"I didn't know that," he continued. "Anyway, I scout the strip clubs and I find her, working at Busteroo's, so I call Harry – Mr. Harrodi – and tell him I found her."

"And?" Kimo said.

"He tells me to keep an eye on her and he'll get back to me in a couple of days."

"Which is why you were following her around, right?" I said.

"Yeah. Just making sure she was following her regular routine, not doing anything unusual, like that."

"So then what happened?" Kimo said.

"A few days go by and Harry calls me again and he tells me that this Buttaree girl was his former girlfriend and she stole some money from him, so he's sending a couple of detectives over here to arrest her."

"He's sending a couple of detectives over here? What is this guy, a cop?"

"No. He runs some kind of entertainment business. I think he's an agent, something like that."

"You don't seem to know much about your client," Kimo said.

"Hey, a couple of thousand dollars for following someone around for a few days – that's all I need to know."

"All right. So then what happened?"

"These two detectives from Los Angeles show up. I picked them up at the airport and took them to their hotel. To tell you the truth –"

"That would be an excellent idea," Kimo said, glancing down at Mangrum's lap, where his left hand cradled the fingers of his injured right hand.

The old guy visibly shuddered when he saw Kimo looking at his fingers. "Yeah, I don't think they were detectives," he said. "They sure didn't look like it. Or talk like it. I think they were mob guys."

"Mob guys? What makes you think that?"

"Well, just the way the whole thing went down. After I took them to Busteroo's to see Buttaree's show and gave them all the info I had on her – her address and all that – they gave me an envelope with a thousand bucks in it and told me to get lost."

"Really?"

"Yeah, really. Plus, they had shiny suits. You know, what is that stuff? Sharkskin? Is that what that material is called? Nobody wears those suits except mob guys. I don't think they even make them any more. Anyway, real shiny. I don't think detectives wear suits that shiny, not even in L.A."

"Whatevahs. So then?"

"You sure you ain't got any aspirin?" Mangrum said. "My hand really hurts."

"I'm sure. Keep talking."

"That's it. I took the money and did like they said. I got lost."

"Wait a second," I said, interrupting again. "When did all this happen?"

"Last week. Early last week. Like, Monday or Tuesday."

"But I saw you on Thursday afternoon, right down here on Kuhio, at the bus stop. That's the night Buttaree was killed, Thursday night. If you were off the case on Monday or Tuesday, what were you doing following her on Thursday?"

"I wasn't following her. I was probably just catching the bus – I live around here."

"Where?"

"On Ala Wai. I usually just walk down to Kuhio and catch the bus into town, or wherever."

It was Kimo's turn to interrupt. "Okay, that explains Thursday. What about now? Why are you in here, searching for ... whatevahs?"

"You know, that's a funny story," Mangrum said.

"Then make me laugh."

"Well, earlier today, I get another call from that guy – Harry. He's heard the news about Buttaree being dead, he says, but he hasn't been able to get in touch with those two detectives he sent over. They checked out of their hotel. He wants me to find them and then let him know what's going on? Another grand for me, he said, although I'll probably have to spend it on doctor's bills." He looked down ruefully at his injured hand.

"So what are you doing in here, searching the place? Did you think those two detectives might be hiding under Buttaree's sink?"

"Well, ... no, ... I didn't think that."

"Then what?"

"I was just looking for clues. Anything that might point me in the right direction, ya know? I don't have any idea where to start looking for those guys."

Apparently sensing that Thomas Mangrum had no more useful information for us, Kimo backed away from the table, pointed at the old man's hand and told him, "You probably should go get that looked at."

"Yeah, I'll be sure to do that. Thanks for the advice!" he said, his voice heavy with cynicism and frustrated anger. "Is that it? Can I go? I really don't know anything else about any of this."

"Yeah, get out of here," Kimo said.

Mangrum struggled to his feet and staggered off toward Buttaree's front door, weaving from side to side and occasionally stumbling. Evidently, when you're older, breaking a finger affects your equilibrium.

We followed him and stood in the doorway of the apartment, watching as he shuffled down the hallway to the elevator and stood there, casting nervous glances in our direction. When a loud *ding!* signaled the elevator's arrival, Kimo called to him, saying, "I better not see you around here again."

"Screw you guys!" he yelled back, then flipped us off – with his left hand, of course – before disappearing into the elevator.

We both laughed.

"I doubt he'll be coming back," Kimo said.

"Yeah, not likely," I agreed.

"You still hungry?"

"Starving."

"So let's go get something to eat."

Chapter Thirteen

We ended up down on Kalakaua Avenue, the main street through Waikiki. Normally, walking along the *mauka* sidewalk – the one across the street from the beach – is pretty difficult. That's mainly because of a cultural difference between visitors from North America and visitors from Japan, the two places that send the most tourists to Hawaii. Canadian and U.S. visitors keep to the right as they walk down the sidewalk, while Japanese tourists keep to the left. So, even though the sidewalks in Waikiki are extra-wide, the result is lines of tourists, completely blocking the sidewalk, attempting to go in one direction while an equal number are trying to move in the opposite direction. It can be pretty interesting to watch, actually, as the zigging and zagging of these groups struggling to move past each other frequently produces humorous outcomes.

However, when you're Kimo's size, things are different. As we headed up the sidewalk toward the center of Waikiki, crowds coming toward us automatically parted to let us through. Very considerate of them, in my opinion. And very convenient. I briefly wondered what would happen if Kimo carried a large spear and kept saying, in a loud voice, "Make a hole! Make a hole!" Probably most folks would be walking on the other side of the street.

Ramen was our consensus dinner choice, and International Market Place was where we got it. After we ate, we crossed the street to the *makai* side – the ocean side – and headed back to my apartment along the wide sidewalk next to the beach. Once you get past the Moana Hotel and the Honolulu Police Department Waikiki Substation, there are no stores or hotels on this side of Kalakaua, so at this time of night – it was almost nine o'clock – the sidewalk was relatively tourist free. A few visitors, still dressed in bathing suits, frolicked beneath the big statue of Duke Kahanamoku, taking pictures and acting stupidly, as many travelers to Waikiki seem inclined to do. Kimo flashed them a *shaka* sign as we walked past and we received a few curious stares in return.

We walked all the way down to Kapahulu Avenue, crossed there and followed Kapahulu up to Kuhio Avenue, where we turned left, backtracking over to Paoakalani, the street where I live. It's a lot longer this way, but it was – as it usually is in Honolulu – a calm, beautiful evening. A gentle breeze swept over the Ko'olau Mountains and down across the city, keeping it at a comfortable temperature with low humidity, just one of the advantages of living on an island in a trade-winds belt. Locals call that breeze, which is a near-constant presence here in the islands, nature's air conditioner.

"Looks like the reporters have given up," Kimo observed when we arrived at my apartment building.

"Well, that's good news, even though they'll probably be back tomorrow. Anyway, let's go get a beer."

"Nah, I'm not coming up."

"Not even one beer?"

"No. One beer will lead to a couple. Plus a joint or two. And the next thing you know, it's one o'clock and I'm still not home. I gotta go to work in the morning."

"'Okay, then. See you on Saturday, I guess."

"Yeah, Saturday."

"You think I should call the police?"

"The police? Why?"

"To tell them about Mangrum," I said.

He thought about it for a while. "Nah, don't bother. I'll tell Pops about it. He'll let them know."

"Great."

"See ya, then."

"Yeah, laters." I watched as he headed up the street toward his 'secret parking spot,' then went inside. It was five past nine.

As soon as I got off the elevator on the fifth floor and headed down the hallway, I saw that something was wrong at Buttaree's apartment. The crime-scene tape Thomas Mangrum had carelessly discarded was now neatly folded and placed in a pile just inside the door, which was open. The lights were on and soft music floated through the open doorway out into the hall.

It seemed unlikely Mangrum would be stupid enough to come back after his earlier experience in that apartment. Perhaps someone new was moving in, although that seemed doubtful, also, considering the fact it wasn't the cops who had originally removed the tape, unblocking the apartment. Or maybe this was the cops, and now they were opening up the place. Then again, cops don't usually play music while they're working. Just to be sure, I decided to check.

I went to the open doorway, knocked loudly on the door, and called, "Hello?"

A tiny, bronze-skinned man dressed in a blue jumpsuit and what looked like a blue shower cap appeared at the end of the short hallway that led to Buttaree's kitchen, followed by an even tinier bronze-skinned woman wearing an identical uniform. Neither of them appeared to be over five feet tall. "Yes?" the tiny man said.

The situation was a little bit awkward – I hadn't really considered what I'd say to whoever I found in the apartment. "Oh. Uh, ... hi," I said. "I live across the hall. I'm Archie." I took a few steps down the hall, toward them.

"Hello, Mr. Archie," the tiny man said.

The tiny woman pressed her hands together and bowed her head slightly in my direction, a common greeting gesture in many parts of Southeast Asia and seen occasionally here in Hawaii.

"I was ... uh, friends with the woman who lived here."

"Yes, yes. Miss Buttaree. So sad," he said.

"So sad," the tiny woman repeated, and shook her head. "We are so sorry."

"Thank you. Are you friends of hers?"

"No, no. We – my wife, Thidapa, and myself – are hired to clean this apartment. I am Kasemchai." This time both he and his wife bowed, so I pressed my hands together and bowed back at them. They both smiled. Whether it was because my gesture had made them happy or whether I had just made a fool of myself, I couldn't tell.

"You're Thai?" I said.

"Yes, yes. From Bangkok." Both of their smiles grew larger, apparently because I recognized their country of origin from their names.

"A beautiful country," I said, although I don't know why I was prolonging this conversation. Now that I knew what was going on at Buttaree's – that Thomas Mangrum hadn't come back – all I really wanted to do was return to my apartment, get a beer, fire up a joint, and relax. I suppose I was just being polite.

"You have been there?" Kasemchai said.

"No. I haven't. But I've heard it's very pretty. And I've seen pictures, too. Many beautiful beaches."

"Yes, yes, very beautiful. Like Hawaii, too." Thidapa nodded her head in apparent agreement.

"Yes. Well, ..." Although I was enjoying, to some degree, our mutual admiration society for each others' homelands, I had the information I needed and had now reached that awkward stage of the conversation where I was searching for a polite way to say goodbye. "So ..."

"You are needing something?" said Kasemchai.

"Well, I left some beer in her refrigerator," I said, although I have no idea why I said that – it wasn't true. I didn't even know if Buttaree had any beer in her fridge. It was just one of those things that popped out of my mouth, apparently without my brain being involved. "I was going to take it back to my place."

"Yes, yes. You take."

"You don't mind?"

"No, no. You take. We are not allowed to take food. All food must be thrown away."

"Oh. Okay, then." I made my way past them and over to the refrigerator.

"You take all food," Thidapa said.

Buttaree's fridge was almost empty. There wasn't much to take – half a loaf of bread, some extremely funky-looking sandwich meat, a can of tuna fish, some mayonnaise, two bottles of beer and a pound of butter. I snatched up the beers and was about to close the door when I thought I heard the butter call to me, in a super-soft voice only I could hear, *"Hey! Take me, too."*

I stared at it. The butter, I mean. Butter doesn't really talk, does it? That had to be my imagination, working overtime. Right? For some reason, the scene from that movie Buttaree and I watched – the one where the bad guy was carving a bar of soap and Buttaree suggested butter would be easier to use – popped into my head,

"I'm going to take this butter, too. Okay?" I said.

"Sure, sure. You take anything," Kasemchai said.

Butter in one hand and beers in the other, I bowed once more to the couple, said goodbye and headed back to my place. I could hardly wait to get back home. That theory Kimo told me about, earlier – the one where Buttaree ended up drowned accidentally while she was being tortured for information – might just be what actually happened. And perhaps the reason the killer couldn't find what he was looking for was that Buttaree hid it in the butter!

Chapter Fourteen

Back at my apartment, I put the beer in the fridge and the 'talking' butter on the counter. The one-pound box the butter came in had already been opened but the box was full – there were still four sticks of butter inside. That was a good sign, in my estimation. I dumped them out.

Upon close examination, it was obvious one of the quarter-pound sticks had been unwrapped and then rewrapped. Also, one side was just a little bit lumpy. Whatever Buttaree had stashed inside – if she'd actually done that – would have to be pretty small. Maybe a key, like in that movie.

I unwrapped the irregularly-wrapped stick of butter and crumbled it into the sink, expecting to find a key or something similarly small, but nothing was inside. It was just butter – clumps of sticky, greasy butter – all over my sink and coating my hands. Disappointment doesn't even begin to describe the way I felt. Just to be on the safe side, I dumped the other three sticks of butter into the sink and, one by one, broke them apart and examined them. Still nothing.

Hmm. Very strange. Clearly someone – presumably Buttaree – had messed with that one stick of butter, unwrapping it and attempting to insert some small object. Apparently, though, she'd been unsuccessful. Was that because that object had been too big to fit? Without knowing what the object was, that question was impossible to answer.

Or maybe Buttaree had succeeded in getting the object into the butter but the murderer found it and removed it. That hypothesis got tossed out almost as quickly as it had appeared in my head. It seemed unlikely – no, impossibly unlikely – that a murdering thief would stick around to reshape a stick of butter, then rewrap it, place it back in the box and return the box to the refrigerator.

So I could come to no conclusion other than that Buttaree, for some unknown reason, had changed her mind. About where to hide the mystery object, I mean. And if she'd changed her mind, then she must have hidden it someplace else. Somewhere in her apartment, most likely.

I scraped the butter chunks out of my sink and put them in the trash, checking again to make sure I hadn't missed anything, then washed the sink and my hands, grabbed a beer and headed for the couch. Perhaps a few tokes of weed would help to clarify the confusion I was feeling. I'd been so sure that stick of butter was going to have a key or some other piece of important evidence hidden inside, yet it didn't. Very disappointing.

The weed did nothing to clear things up, but after a half-dozen hits or so, I felt pretty relaxed. Well, extremely relaxed, actually. I slouched down in my seat, leaned my head back and closed my eyes, intending to zone out for 10 or 15 minutes and let myself unwind from the stress I'd been feeling lately. That was at about ten-thirty.

At five past two I awoke suddenly. My back hurt, my neck was stiff, and my beer – still three-quarters full – was warm. I staggered into the kitchen, massaging my neck as I went, and splashed some water on my face. Then, new beer in hand, I returned to the couch, took a couple of hits from the joint and several long pulls on the beer, and went back to thinking about the situation in which I now found myself.

It was ridiculous to think I killed Buttaree. The cops were making a big mistake if they thought they were going to pin her murder on me, at least in my opinion. The explanation of what really happened that made the most sense to me was Pops' theory that she'd been drowned accidentally. The murderer was trying to get her to tell him where she had hidden … something – the money Thomas Mangrum said she stole in L.A., most likely.

I really liked that theory. Unfortunately, the police did not. They apparently were leaning toward the wannabe-boyfriend-gets-rejected-and-kills-her explanation of the crime. And that wannabe boyfriend was me!

The way to change the cops' minds seemed pretty obvious, though – find whatever Buttaree had hidden and show it to them. Of course, the police had already searched her apartment pretty thoroughly, I imagined. But they'd been looking for clues related to her murder – trying to figure out exactly what happened, why it happened, and who did it. They had not yet come up with the theory – now discarded, regrettably – that Buttaree was being tortured for information, and I'm almost certain they didn't conduct a search for something she might have hidden.

It was also possible the killer had searched the place and found what he was looking for, I suppose, but I doubted it. More likely was that, after accidentally killing her, his main concern was to get out of that apartment as soon as possible. There really was only one way to know for sure – another search, this time looking for something small another to be considered for hiding in a stick of butter. A key would be my guess.

However, convincing the police to conduct a second search – this time for something that might not even exist – seemed unrealistic. Especially since, according to Kimo, they'd already made up their minds that I was the killer!

Maybe the Thai couple, Kasemchai and Thidapa, would find whatever-it-was while they were cleaning the apartment. Or had already found it. I wondered what they'd do if they did find something. Would they keep it? Turn it over to the cops? Probably not – it wouldn't mean anything to them. The odds were they'd just throw it out along with the other trash they'd collected.

To be sure, that outcome also seemed fairly far-fetched. If Buttaree had gone to the trouble of finding a good hiding place – and it appeared she had – it was improbable to think a routine cleaning of the apartment would turn up the missing piece of evidence that would prove I wasn't a murderer.

I took a hit, placed the half-smoked joint on the rim of the ashtray and held in the smoke while I considered what to do next. This whole thing – me sitting here trying to figure out my next move – was really just an exercise in procrastination, I eventually decided. I knew what needed to be done because, having eliminated all other options, there was only one logical course of action left. If I wanted a second search of Buttaree's apartment to be conducted, I was going to have to do it myself.

Chapter Fifteen

Tuesday morning, 2:45 A.M. HST

A quick look through my peephole showed the corridor outside my apartment to be calm and quiet. It usually is at this time of the morning. I cracked open my door and looked out.

The door to Buttaree's apartment was closed and the crime-scene tape had been replaced over it, indicating Kasemchai and his wife had finished cleaning the place and left. Perfect. I let myself out and crossed over to her place.

It was a little spooky – okay, a lot spooky – breaking into a place where someone had just been murdered, made even more so by the fact that it was almost three o'clock in the morning. I pulled off the crime-scene tape, piled it neatly to one side, pushed open the door and went in, pulling the door shut behind me.

Religion has never been a big part of my life and I haven't really decided what I believe, especially that part about what happens after you die. And as for whether or not ghosts, or spirits, or whatever you want to call them, exist, well, ... I haven't made up my mind about that, either. Although I've never seen a ghost, I've heard plenty of stories about them – nearly all of them scary in nature – so I'm not sure what's true and what isn't. But, belief in ghosts or not, the hair on the back of my neck was standing up and a strong urge to pee had suddenly appeared.

The inside of the apartment smelled of cleaning solution and Thai food – apparently Kasemchai and Thidapa had made themselves a little snack before they left. A small amount of light from a street lamp leaked through the kitchen window and illuminated the rest of the apartment in a pale glow. Not wanting to conduct my search in near-darkness, I turned on the overhead kitchen light.

The layout of Buttaree's apartment was the same as mine, only reversed – a combination kitchen/dining room and a living room at one end with a bedroom at the opposite end, the two ends separated by a short hallway and an extra-large bathroom. In the living room, double-wide glass doors led to a lanai, which added a nice local touch as well as providing a lovely view of surrounding high-rises. Since I was already in the kitchen, that seemed as good a place as any to start my search.

Actually, there wasn't much to search. The Thai cleaning crew had left the place in spotless condition. Everything except tableware and a few kitchen utensils had been removed. The unplugged refrigerator was empty and so clean it appeared new. Kasemchai and Thidapa had done a bang-up job on that.

I pulled the refrigerator out and checked behind it, finding nothing. The stove, however, refused to move away from its cozy spot next to the wall when I attempted the same maneuver. No matter how hard I pulled, it spurned my efforts, so I crawled up on top of it and peered down over the back, examining both it and the wall behind it. Again, nothing.

The same was true as I made my way around the apartment, examining the undersides of chairs, tables, the bed, lamps – basically, anything that wasn't nailed down. I found nothing. Zilch. No clues, no small keys – nada.

Disappointed, I slumped into a living room chair to consider what to do next. I'd already searched every place I could think of where Buttaree might have hidden ... well, whatever it was. If it even existed, that is, of which I was beginning to have serious doubts. And then, as I sat there feeling sorry for myself and bummed out at my lack of success,

I noticed the dark red drapes that covered the glass doors leading out onto the lanai.

They were the same type of drapes as in my apartment – same material, same color, same style. Not surprising. At one time all 28 apartments in this building looked exactly alike, and some of the short-term rentals, such as Buttaree's place, still perpetuated the original look. I made a mental note to check into the cost of new drapes.

But these drapes, despite being identical to the ones in my apartment, somehow looked different. I stared at them, trying to find some small dissimilarity that would explain why. And then I saw it – these drapes hung much farther away from the lanai doors than did the ones in my apartment. They stood out from the wall, made possible by a 90 degree bend of perhaps four inches at each end. The drapes in my apartment were much closer to the lanai doors.

A closer examination disclosed the reason for the disparity. Behind the drapes were vertical, wide-slatted, free-hanging, white plastic venetian blinds, suspended from a long, square, white metal tube above the doorway. Nothing hung between the drapes and the glass doors in my apartment, which is why my drapes were so much closer to the doors.

My inspection also produced another, even more interesting disclosure – end caps. Each end of the square metal tube was covered by a plastic cap that covered the open tube. Hence, the term – end cap. And upon further investigation, I saw that one of these end caps was damaged. It looked as if someone had removed it using a screwdriver or some similar implement and, in the process, had left long scratches on the outside.

Could this be it? Could the evidence I'd been searching for, but had just about given up hope of ever finding, be inside that innocent-looking square tube? I removed the drapes and, with considerable difficulty, wrestled the entire venetian blind assembly down onto the living room floor.

The damaged end cap was the object of my attention, but when I tried to pull it off, it wouldn't budge. Whoever had removed and replaced it – that would have been Buttaree, hopefully – hadn't done a very good job, especially when they put it back. It appeared to have been hammered on at a slightly crooked angle, resulting in an end cap that was wedged solidly onto the square tube and did not want to leave.

That was the bad news. The good news was, since the end cap was made of plastic, it didn't stand a chance against my pocket knife. While my knife wasn't big, it was sharp. I dug it out of my pocket and began cutting away one corner of the end cap, intending to free it.

For an end cap, though, this one was particularly stubborn. It did not want to let go of the tube it covered. As I looked at a couple of the small pieces I'd cut off, I saw why. Whoever had replaced it had added glue to the mix – the entire cap was stuck solidly to the square tube and wasn't about to be removed.

That turned out to be a fairly easy problem to solve, actually. I found a serrated steak knife in a kitchen drawer and used it to cut through the tube about a half-inch past the end cap. The metal was thin but it still took me quite a while. When I had three sides of the tube cut, I bent the cap end back, lifted up the long end of the tube and tapped the now-open end on the floor. A small pink envelope, rolled up and wrapped with a rubber band, slid out.

I stared at it. This was it. This was what I'd been searching for – evidence. Evidence that would clear me as a suspect in Buttaree's murder. Maybe. Hopefully.

The envelope, once freed from the constraints of the rubber band and unrolled, revealed it's contents – a flash drive and a small, bronze-colored key. Stamped onto the key were the letters K.K. and the number 31. My hand started to tremble slightly as I gazed at what

I hoped would turn out to be evidence that I wasn't a murderer. And then, I started to smile.

A rush of what could only be called joy swept over me as I contemplated those two small items. I felt like dancing. Or doing cartwheels. Or something! However, at the same time, that little voice inside my head was saying, *C'mon, you got what you were looking for. Let's get out of here!* I decided to take my little voice's advice.

I pulled out my key ring and added the bronze key to the six other keys already on it. Those would be the keys to my front door, my car, a storage locker downstairs in the garage, the mail box in the lobby, a gym locker key I was supposed to have returned about three years ago when I dropped my membership, and one other key that had been on there for so long I couldn't remember what it fit. An old padlock I could no longer find was my best guess.

With the key ring and the flash drive safely secured in my pocket, I turned out the lights and exited the apartment. Someone else could worry about fixing the venetian blinds and the drapes. Right now I was eager to get back to my place and see what was on that flash drive. It would probably be a good idea also to make a copy for myself, so I'd have a backup, as proof. Then, later in the day, after I got some sleep, I'd give that cop, Detective Higa, a call and let him know what I'd found.

Chapter Sixteen

The lock on Buttaree's door was still broken and I couldn't get the door to stay closed. I was bent over, fiddling with it, when down the hallway the elevator arrived with a ding. I checked my watch – 5:57 – wondering who could be coming home at this time of the morning. Although there were four apartments on each floor, I barely knew the occupants of the other two units. With me working nights and they being day-workers, I rarely even saw them, and when I did, our interactions usually consisted of little more than a smile, a nod, and a, Hey! Howzit?

But it wasn't neighbors stepping out of the elevator – it was cops. Two of them, to be exact. I stood up to greet them as they headed down the corridor toward me. Meanwhile, my brain frantically scrambled for a logical explanation of what I was doing in front of Buttaree's apartment, tampering with the lock.

I recognized one of the two officers – Officer Jenkins, the tall, freckle-faced haole cop who'd responded to my call to the police the first night Buttaree showed up at my apartment, naked, wet, and afraid. The other officer was new, a dark, heavy-set, middle-aged man whose name tag identified him as Officer Mauga, a Samoan name.

Officer Jenkins recognized me, as well. "Mr. Morris," he said. "What are you doing?"

My brain had given up on attempts to come up with a reasonable explanation of what I was doing out here, in front of Buttaree's apartment, fooling around with her front door at six in the morning, so I decided to fess up. "I was conducting a search," I explained.

"A search?" Officer Jenkins said. "Of Miss Gudnis' place?"

"Yeah."

"We had a noise complaint. Someone was doing construction work inside the apartment at five o'clock this morning."

"That was me, I guess."

"What were you searching for?" Officer Mauga said.

I reached into my pocket and pulled out the flash drive. "This," I said, and handed it over to Officer Jenkins. "It was hidden in the venetian blinds that cover the doors to the lanai." For some reason, I didn't feel the need to mention the key that safely resided on my key ring.

"What is it?" he said, holding it in his palm and looking at it.

"It's a flash drive."

Officer Jenkins smiled. "I know that. But why were you searching for it? What's its significance?"

"Oh. Well, have you been keeping up with this case? This murder?"

"Not that much. I was interviewed by Detective Higa, answered a few questions, and I saw a couple of articles in the paper. That's about it. Why?"

"Do you know they think I killed her? You guys. The police, I mean."

"I've heard that theory. But I think I heard it on TV, not from the police."

"How about that other one? The one that says she was killed accidentally while she was being tortured for information. Have you heard about that?"

"No, I don't think I have." He handed the flash drive to Officer Mauga, who bounced it up and down on his palm a few times while he stared at it. "Whose theory is that?"

"It was one of the theories the police had," I said.

"Had?"

"Yeah, past tense. They gave it up to concentrate on proving I did it."

"I've heard that theory," Officer Mauga said, still juggling the flash drive. "It was an accident."

Officer Jenkins reached out with one hand and caught the flash drive on a bounce, taking it back from his partner. "What kind of information do you think this ... murderer was trying to extract from her, anyway?" he said.

"Well, according to Thomas Mangrum, she stole a bunch of money from some guy on the mainland and he was trying to get it back."

"Mangrum?" the two cops exchanged glances.

"Yeah. You know him?"

"Old guy? Gray hair, aloha shirt, blue Detroit Tigers cap? Claims he's a private eye? That Thomas Mangrum?"

"He's not a private eye?" I said.

"He used to be. Years ago. But he's not licensed now. How do you know him, anyway?"

I described what had happened earlier that evening – technically, the night before, I guess – explaining who Kimo was but leaving out the part about how he got Mangrum to talk by breaking his finger.

"And that's what you were looking for? The missing money?"

"No. Not really. Both the police and Mangrum had already searched the place, so I figured it had to be something small. Like that," I said, pointing at the flash drive.

Officer Jenkins turned to his partner and said, "Nolan, go check out the place, will you?"

Officer Mauga nodded, said, "Sure," and disappeared into Buttaree's apartment.

"So, is this it? Is this all you found?" Officer Jenkins said, holding up the flash drive.

For some reason, that little voice in my head was screaming at me. *Don't tell him about the key! Don't mention it!* "Yeah, that's it," I said, hoping I sounded truthful.

"You're going to have to come with us. Down to the station." He handed the flash drive back to me. "You can turn this in when they interview you."

"Am I under arrest?"

"No. Not yet, anyway. That will be up to someone else, not us. I wouldn't worry about it, though. You probably won't be arrested, considering the circumstances."

"Which are – ?"

"You know – that you were just trying to prove your innocence. That you didn't kill your girlfriend."

"She wasn't my girlfriend," I said.

"Yeah, I meant ... your friend."

"Friend, yes. Girlfriend, no."

Officer Mauga returned from his inspection of the apartment. "It's like he said, Benny. It was hidden in the blinds," he told his partner. He turned to me. "You made one big mess in there."

"Sorry. No tools." I hoped that would explain the shambles I'd left behind.

"Okay, let's go," Officer Jenkins said.

As we rode down in the elevator, I couldn't help but wonder if my trip to the police station would be on the back of a bicycle. I supposed it was even possible, since it wasn't that far, that I'd have to walk. I needn't have worried, though – a police car was waiting in front of the building, ready to provide transportation. Officer Mauga held the door open for me. Light was just beginning to leak into the city from the east, out past Koko Head way, as I climbed into the back seat for the five-minute journey to the Waikiki substation.

Chapter Seventeen

The Waikiki substation was practically empty. A sunburned tourist was complaining loudly to a bored-looking desk clerk that his wallet had been stolen, and the blonde young woman next to him was protesting, just as loudly, that she wasn't the one who took it. The girl was obviously a prostitute – she was wearing a skirt about six inches long, a halter top that showed a good 75% of her boobs, and the stiletto heels of her shoes were longer than her skirt. If you walk down Kalakaua Avenue late in the evening, you'll encounter a half-dozen or more nearly-identical young women, standing around, soliciting Asian tourists for "dates." I sat on a bench and watched them as Officers Jenkins and Mauga spoke with the only other officer in the place, presumably about me.

After several minutes, Officer Jenkins came over to me and said, "They're sending someone to pick you up."

"Pick me up? What happens then?"

Officer Jenkins smiled and shrugged. "Not sure, really. They'll probably take you down to the main station, interview you and then decide whether to charge you or not. That's what usually happens."

"Great," I said.

"So, can we trust you to wait here and not leave?"

"I don't suppose I could go get some breakfast and then come back, could I? I'm kinda hungry."

He shook his head and smiled again. "Sorry. You have to wait here."

"Okay then, I guess."

"Try to stay out of trouble, Mr. Morris."

"It's Archie. Nobody calls me Mr. Morris."

"All right. Try to stay out of trouble, Archie. Leave the investigating up to the police."

"Yeah. That's what I intend to do from now on."

"Good." He headed back over to where his partner was waiting and the two of them left.

As I watched them leave, I decided that, for cops, they were pretty decent, just trusting me to sit and wait for some other officer to come and take me away to be arrested. That was probably because we were in Waikiki, where most people who come in contact with the police are tourists, and where it appears the cops have been ordered to enforce the laws in a kindly, friendly fashion. Treating our valuable visitors in any other manner would be bad for Hawaii's hospitality industry and our reputation as a carefree, fun-filled vacation spot. Which is just my way of saying that you can get away with things in Waikiki that would be frowned upon in other parts of Honolulu.

Still, I couldn't help but think that if I'd left the investigating to the police, the way Officer Jenkins wanted, I'd probably be a lot closer to being charged with Buttaree's murder. If I was judging the situation correctly – and I believed I was – the cops had pretty much made up their minds that I was their guy and were out to prove it. If anyone was going to prove I was innocent, it was likely going to have to be me.

Of course, I wasn't completely alone in this – Kimo was on my side, for sure. And Pops would make a great character witness, if I ever needed one, what with him being an ex-cop and a high-ranking one, at that. Pops has known me for practically my entire life. I was pretty sure he'd tell them I couldn't possibly be a murderer. I was just too nice a guy.

I briefly turned my attention back to the tourist and the hooker, who were now arguing loudly about some missing money. Apparently, the tourist dude's wallet had somehow magically reappeared. But ... it was, according to him, short approximately $1600 and his credit cards, and he was less than thrilled about that. I watched them argue for a couple of minutes, then got bored, leaned my head back against the wall and closed my eyes.

The fact I'd been without sleep for a long, long time suddenly occurred to me and with it came the realization I was tired – very tired. I wiggled myself into a semi-comfortable position, took a deep breath and blew out all the anxiety I was feeling. Then I did something I've always been good at – I fell asleep.

I was still asleep when Detective Higa woke me up at a quarter to nine.

"Mr. Morris?" he said, shaking me slightly by my shoulder.

I opened my eyes, blinked at him a couple of times, yawned and said, "It's Archie."

"Archie. Yes. I need you to come with me." He turned and headed toward the exit without waiting for me, so I got up and shambled after him, still yawning.

Outside, it was another beautiful day in paradise – warm, sunny, the trade winds just beginning to blow so that it was warm and cool at the same time. The sidewalk was already filled with smiling and laughing tourists dressed in bathing suits or other casual attire, snapping pictures with their phones as they made their way to the beach to work on their sunburns. There's a tendency for locals to take our weather for granted, but the visitors who pay thousands of dollars to spend a week or two here know – Hawaii has the best weather in the world!

Detective Higa's car was parked in front, on Kalakaua, part of a short line of police cars, but his was an older Buick sedan, gray in color and not a blue-and-white. He held open the passenger-side door for me and I got in. "Fasten your seat belt," he said as he closed the door.

I did as he said, watching him as he walked around the front of his car and got in the driver's side. He was wearing shorts, slippahs and an aloha shirt, so evidently this – him picking me up, I mean – was either being done on his own time or Honolulu police detectives are allowed to dress any way they like.

"You hungry?" he said, fastening his seat belt.

"Yeah, starving. And I gotta pee like a racehorse!"

He laughed. "I know just the place, then."

'Just the place' was McDonald's, up the street a ways and around the corner on Liliuokalani Avenue. Detective Higa parked in front, stuck an official *Honolulu Police – Official Business* card on his dash and said, "Let's go eat."

After taking a leak and then chowing down on a couple of Egg McMuffins and a large cup of black coffee, I felt a lot better as I climbed back into the detective's Buick. Not better about my situation, perhaps, but physically better. I've suspected for a long time that if there were no coffee to start my day, my day would never start.

"Fasten your seat belt," Detective Higa said again, and again I did as he said. Actually, he didn't have to remind me. I always buckle up when I'm in a car.

We went up to the corner and turned right on Kuhio, heading toward Diamond Head. When it dead-ended at Kapahulu Avenue, we turned left, went up to Paki Avenue and turned right, following Paki past Kapiolani Park until we picked up Diamond Head Road.

There wasn't much conversation as we drove along, except for once when Detective Higa commented, "It's a beautiful day," and I replied, "Yeah, just like always."

We continued along Diamond Head Road, which winds around the front and part of the back side of the crater. I wondered where we were going – this was not the way to the main police station. We passed the lookout, where several cars had pulled over to allow their occupants to gaze out over the Pacific and take pictures. On a clear day, you can just make out the island of Molokai, roughly 20 miles off to the east. Unfortunately, it was a hazy morning, and all that could be seen from the lookout on this day was miles of blue water.

Shortly past the lookout we encountered Fort Ruger Park, a small patch of greenery not much bigger than my apartment, and were confronted with a choice – veer left and continue circling around the crater on Diamond Head Road or go straight, down Kahala Avenue toward Waialae Golf Course. Detective Higa turned left.

It had been a while, maybe years, since I'd been out this way. Not much had changed, though. This side of Leahi Crater – the real name of Diamond Head – was less than impressive. It looked like the back side of any hill. And it was dotted with houses, something not allowed on the opposite side of the crater, where preserving the iconic view of Diamond Head was a high priority.

I was puzzled about where we were going and that Detective Higa had so little to tell me. Was there something he wanted to bring up but just couldn't find the right time to do it? Or did he think the tactic of him not saying much might cause me to fill in the silence, maybe even by confessing? That wasn't going to happen. I decided to ask him what was going on. "Where are you taking me, anyway?" I said.

"Home," he replied. Not really much of a talker, this guy.

"Kinda the long way, isn't it?"

"That's okay. I get paid by the hour."

I looked over at him. He wasn't smiling and I couldn't tell if he was kidding or not with that remark.

We continued up and around the crater until we got to the high point of the back side, just past Kapiolani Community College. It's somewhere along this stretch that Diamond Head Road, for some inexplicable reason, suddenly becomes Monsarrat Avenue, which leads downhill into Waikiki. When I was a kid, I used to walk down Monsarrat on my way to Waikiki Elementary School. Kimo and I used to call it Monster Rat Avenue – we thought that was pretty funny.

As we started down the hill, back toward my place, we went past Trousseau Street. I pointed off to the right. "I grew up over there," I said. "On Wela Street."

"I know," he said. "I know a lot about you, Archie."

Of course you do, I thought. You're a detective. "So ... you're not going to arrest me?"

"Nope."

"What, then?"

"I was told you found something."

"That's right. A flash drive."

"That's it? A flash drive?"

For just a second, the notion that I should tell Detective Higa about the key popped into my head, but then it popped right back out and I decided to keep that information to myself, at least for the time being. "Yeah. It was wrapped up in an envelope, hidden inside the venetian blinds that cover the lanai doors."

"What did you do with it?"

"Nothing. It's in my pocket."

"I wanna take a look at it. See what's on it."

"Oh. Sure, okay." I paused for a bit and then said, "Do you really get paid by the hour?"

He glanced at me and grinned. "Yeah. I really do. I get a car allowance, too."

Chapter Eighteen

We parked across the street from my apartment and went upstairs. The reporters who had been hanging around the front of the building were gone, I was happy to see. Perhaps some new horrific crime had come along to replace the Buttaree story – which had dominated the news over the past few days – and drawn them away.

The crime-scene tape was still piled next to the door of Buttaree's apartment and the door had swung open a few inches. Detective Higa nodded in that direction and said, "Did you do that?"

"I took the tape down, yeah. But the door was already damaged. It won't stay shut."

"The murderer did that, I suppose."

"Yeah."

Once inside my apartment, I got my laptop, turned it on and handed it to Detective Higa, who had taken a seat on the couch. In my spot! I decided not to say anything about that. Instead, I dug the flash drive out of my pocket, gave it to him and went into the kitchen to make coffee.

While I waited for the coffee, I went back into the living room and joined the detective on the couch. It felt a little weird and uncomfortable to be sitting in the spot usually occupied by guests, like I didn't quite fit. *Deal with it*, the little voice in my head told me.

"Finding anything interesting?" I said.

"They're business records. From California. From some guy named Richard Harrodi, who does business under the name, Harry Dick Productions."

"Hairy Dick Productions?" I said, suppressing a chuckle. "That's the name of his company?"

Detective Higa frowned at me. "It's Harry, not Hairy. Harry Dick Productions."

I couldn't help it – I laughed. "Sounds the same to me."

He frowned at me again and went back to examining the contents of the flash drive.

When the coffee was ready, I poured two cups and took them into the living room, setting one in front of Detective Higa. "Black, just the way you like it," I said. Or at least, that's the way he liked it when we were at McDonald's.

"Thanks," he said, without looking up. And then, "This is pretty interesting stuff."

"Yeah?"

"Yeah. It appears this Mr. Harrodi produces pornographic movies under the name Harry Dick Productions."

"That *is* interesting," I said.

"That's not the interesting part," he corrected me. "There are two sets of books on here, both for the same period of time and different from each other."

"Which means –?"

"That Mr. Harrodi is a crook. A tax cheat."

"Wow, this is great news."

"How so?" he said, glancing over at me.

"Well, it backs up the theory that whoever killed Buttaree did it accidentally while they were trying to get her to tell them where this – this flash drive – was hidden. The current theory, as I understand it, is that I killed her because she spurned my romantic overtures."

"It could still be you, Archie," he said. "You could have been the one trying to get the information out of Buttaree and accidentally drowned her."

"But I didn't. Why would I even be interested in this hard drive? With information about some business in California? I don't know anyone in California."

"No?"

"No!"

"What about Thurgood?"

"Who?" And who the hell would name an innocent baby Thurgood, anyway, I wondered.

"Your cousin on your father's side, Thurgood Morris," he said.

Oh. That Thurgood. But no one ever called him that – his name is, and always has been, Tubby. Tubby Morris. So called because of his love of baths as a child. I knew why his real name was Thurgood, though. It was for the same reason my real first name is Meredith. Money. Name your kid after a rich relative and maybe someday he'll inherit a bunch of their moolah. It worked for me.

"I haven't heard from him in years. Maybe a card at Christmas – I'm not even sure about that. Besides, he lives in Las Vegas, not California."

"He moved to Los Angeles three years ago."

"You don't say. I didn't know that." I'd been wondering what Detective Higa had been doing since our interview that first night – the night of Buttaree's murder. Now I knew. He'd been checking up on me, even to the point of knowing more about my mainland relatives than I did, apparently.

"His wife left him."

"Yeah?" I didn't know about that, either. It was easy to lose touch with what was happening on the mainland, being so far away. And Tubby's family and mine were never really that close, anyway.

"Yeah."

"Is he … involved in this, somehow?"

"No." He went back to studying the contents of the flash drive.

My attention wandered over to the ashtray, sitting on the coffee table directly in front of Detective Higa. A half-smoked joint, perched on the edge, stared at me, backed up by an abundance of roaches in the ashtray. Not really a good look, considering the circumstances, I decided.

"I'm going to get some more coffee," I said, getting to my feet. "Want some?"

"No, I'm good."

Thinking he wasn't paying attention, I leaned down and picked up my cup in one hand and the ashtray in the other and headed for the kitchen.

"I don't care about that," he said.

"What?"

"Pakalolo. I don't care. You wanna smoke, that's your business."

"Good to know," I called from the kitchen. I filled my cup and returned to the living room.

"I'm gonna have to take this with me," Detective Higa said.

"The flash drive?"

"Yeah. I've gotta have an expert look at it. Someone who understands this stuff. I'm a homicide detective, not an accountant."

"Okay, I guess." It wasn't as if I had much of a choice in the matter.

"I can copy it for you, if you want. Onto your hard drive."

"Yeah, all right. Do that," I said, although I doubted it would be much good to me. I wasn't an accountant, either. Still, I supposed it was a good idea to have a copy, if only as proof that I was once in possession of the flash drive.

By the time Detective Higa left, it was almost noon. I'd been up for two days straight and was beginning to feel the effects of going without sleep for so long. The short nap I'd had at the Waikiki substation had done little to refresh me, and even the coffee I'd consumed was doing nothing to help me stay awake. I dragged myself into my bedroom and crashed onto my bed. Things were bound to be better by the time I awoke, I told myself just before falling into a deep, dreamless sleep.

Chapter Nineteen

It was almost seven o'clock when I woke up. I felt terrible. My unusual sleeping habits of the last couple of days had caught up to me. More sleep was probably what I needed, and while that seemed like a good plan, my stomach had other ideas. Food.

A quick shower helped to refresh me and I found some leftover chicken in my fridge. It had been in there for a while – maybe four or five days – but it passed the sniff test so I decided to eat it. I heated it up in the microwave and had it for dinner, along with some slightly stale bread and a beer. After eating, I went into the living room, lit up an after-dinner joint and grabbed my computer. There was research to be done.

The research involved the key I'd found with the flash drive, specifically, the initials stamped on the key, K.K. I needed to find out what those two letters – which are among the more common consonants in the admittedly-short Hawaiian alphabet – stood for. Of course, Buttaree might have brought the key with her from the mainland, in which case it would have nothing to do with anything in Hawaii and would be of no use in proving my innocence. Hopefully, that wouldn't be the case.

Anyway, I had to start somewhere, and, since Google knows everything, I started my search there. A lot of street names in Hawaii start with the letter K, so I began by trying a few of those. Kapahulu, Kapiolani, Ke'eaumoku, Kalanianaole and a few more brought no useful results. I decided to do what I should have done in the first place – just ask Google if it knew what the initials K.K. stood for.

I typed in, *What does K.K. mean on Oahu?* and Google immediately responded with 10,900,000 results. However, only three of them actually seemed to be located on Oahu – Kama'aina Kites, Kehau's Kookies, and Kozy Keeps Mini-Storage. And of the three, Kozy Keeps was by far the most promising.

A box on the right of my screen told me the basic facts about Kozy Keeps – mini-lockers available in three different sizes starting at $10 a month, open from 9 A.M. To 9 P.M. at 27 locations on Oahu. And one of those locations was not far away, on Kapahulu Avenue.

I took a hit off the joint and leaned back to consider my findings. It was dead certain that Buttaree had taken advantage of Kozy Keeps' advertised low, low prices – otherwise, there'd be no key. And since she didn't have a car, it seemed logical to think she'd pick the branch closest to her, the Kapahulu branch. From here, it would be just a leisurely 10 to 15 minute walk or maybe a 3-minute taxi or Uber ride away.

One thing I was pretty sure of – Buttaree wasn't storing personal belongings at Kozy Keeps. You don't glue the key to your locker inside a venetian blinds hanger if all that's in the locker are some photos of an old boyfriend, or costume jewelry, or, as we like to say here in Hawaii, *whatevah*! The content of that locker was obviously something she didn't want found, and most likely it was also what got her killed. If I had to guess, I'd say it was probably the money she reportedly stole from Richard Harrodi, AKA Harry Dick.

It was too late to do anything about Kozy Keeps and Buttaree's locker, so I made a mental note to check it out the following day, got myself a beer and called Kimo, intending to bring him up to date on the latest information about the case.

"Wassup?" came the familiar voice of Pops, Kimo's dad.

"Hey, Pops. Howzit?"

"Pretty good on this end. Not so much for you, though, huh?"

"Yeah, that's putting it mildly. Is Kimo around?" I figured Kimo had to be somewhere close by – we were talking on his phone.

"He's in the shower."

"In your shower?"

"Yeah, the water's off at his place."

"I'm surprised be fits."

Pops laughed. "He has to duck down to wash his hair, you know."

I knew that already but I laughed along with him. "So ... tell him I called, okay?"

"Sure, Archie. Listen, are you okay?"

"Whaddaya mean?"

"You know, with all this stuff going on. You being the main suspect in your girlfriend's murder and all the crap that's on the TV and in the paper."

"She wasn't my girlfriend, Pops. And I definitely didn't kill her."

"Yeah, yeah, I know that, Archie. I know you couldn't kill anyone. But that's what everyone thinks. And the police ..."

"Yeah? The police ... what?"

"Well, I hear things, you know? Down at the station."

"What kind of things, Pops? What do you hear?"

"That the investigation's over. You know Amos Higa?"

"The detective who's been investigating Buttaree's death, right?"

"Yeah. He turned everything over to the prosecutor and caught a new case. He's finished with you."

"What's that mean, exactly? Is that good news or bad news for me?"

"What I heard is that the prosecutor is going to present your case to the grand jury. Next Tuesday, I think."

"So, ... ?"

"That's bad news."

"Really?"

"Yeah. It means the prosecutor thinks you're guilty."

"You know, I found some new evidence and gave it to Detective Higa."

"Yeah. A flash drive, right? Higa thinks that points away from you and toward someone else killing her, but the prosecutor thinks it proves you did it."

"How is that possible?" I said.

"He thinks you drowned her trying to get her to tell you where the flash drive was hidden, and the proof is that you went back, searched the apartment and found it."

"But I turned it over to the police right away. Or tried to, anyway."

"Because you got caught burglarizing her apartment. Right?"

"I wasn't burglarizing it, I was just conducting a different kind of search than the police had done – looking for something Buttaree might have hidden. I always planned to turn over whatever I found to the police." *Except for the key*, said that little voice in my head.

"I see. Well, that probably wasn't a good idea. You should let us – the police, I mean – do the investigating."

Yeah, right. That was the same advice I'd received from just about every cop I'd spoken to recently. I wanted to point out that if it hadn't been for my search, no one would even know about the flash drive and its apparently-useless-to-me contents. Instead, I said, "Anyway, it's up to the grand jury to decide, right?"

Pops chuckled. "You'd think so, wouldn't you? But that's not how it works – grand juries just rubber stamp whatever cases the prosecutor presents to them."

"So what happens then?"

"Ordinarily the suspect is indicted and arrested and then there's a hearing where they set bond."

"Sounds terrific," I said in my best cynical voice. "So, how much will the bail be? Do you know?"

"I'm sorry, Archie. Murderers don't usually get granted bail."

"No?"

"Nope."

"What, then?"

"Off to jail, I'm afraid."

Well, this conversation was not having a positive effect on my disposition. I'd been feeling pretty good about the way things had been going, convinced my discovery would drive suspicion away from me and onto someone else – probably those two missing 'detectives' from L.A. But now it looked as if the cops had found a different fall guy, someone they could blame for the murder – me! "You know any good lawyers?" I said. "Da cheap kine lawyer?"

"Wait and see what happens, Archie. The grand jury doesn't meet until next week – you've still got time. Something could turn up."

"How? How's that gonna happen if nobody's working on this case anymore?"

"Yeah ... well, you never know. Sometimes things show up at the last minute that completely change cases. I know – it happened to me dozens of times."

"Yeah?"

"Yeah. And don't worry about lawyers. If you get indicted, they'll come running to you. This is gonna be a big-time case if you plead innocent."

I didn't like the sound of that. "Of course I'm gonna plead innocent, Pops. Because I am innocent!"

"I know that, Archie. Trust me, this'll all work itself out. Just be patient and let the system do its job. And in the meantime, stay out of whatsername's apartment."

"Buttaree."

"Yeah, Buttaree. Stay out of her place and just wait and see what happens."

"That's exactly what I'm gonna do, Pops."

"Good."

"Anyway, I gotta run," I said.

"You want me to have Kimo call you back?"

"Nah, just tell him I called. Nothing important. I'll see him on Saturday." There didn't seem to be any point in rehashing the same information with Kimo that I'd just discussed with his dad. If Pops knew all this stuff about Buttaree's case, I was pretty sure Kimo did, too.

"Okay. Talk to you later, then. And remember my advice, Archie, 'cause you never know what might happen." He hung up.

Yup, you never know. Maybe not, but I knew one thing – I did not want to go to jail. And if there was anything I could do to prevent that from happening, I was definitely going to do it!

Chapter Twenty

Wednesday

Going to bed at the ridiculously-early time of five past midnight led to me waking up at the equally ridiculously-early time of seven o'clock in the morning. These were not the sleeping hours I was used to. I tossed and turned and pounded my pillow into various odd shapes but was unable to get back to sleep, so I got up and made coffee.

While I waited for my coffee, I sat on the couch and lit up a joint. My big plan for the day was to check out the Kozy Keeps store on Kapahulu Avenue, but that would have to wait until after nine, when they opened. In the meantime, I could ... well, I didn't actually know what I could do. I wasn't used to being up at this time of day, what with being a night-worker who usually got up around noon. Other than getting ready for work – if you had a day job – there didn't seem to be much to do at this time of day.

When the coffee was ready, I made a cup and turned on the TV, but after channel surfing for a few minutes and finding nothing that interested me, I turned it back off. I've always considered myself to be a night person – I never did like mornings – and getting up early on a Wednesday morning just reinforced something I'd suspected for most of my life. For me, mornings suck.

I passed the time speculating on what I might find at Kozy Keeps, and then wondering about the how of it all. How, exactly, was I going to get into Buttaree's locker? Just having a key wouldn't be enough – obviously, some kind of identification would be needed. Identification that I didn't have.

Maybe I could bribe an employee, I thought. Yeah, that might work, especially if I coupled it with a story about Buttaree being a relative – my cousin, perhaps – who was unexpectedly called to the mainland and had asked me to retrieve the contents of her locker for her. Maybe a story like that plus, say, a hundred-dollar bribe would get me into the locker area without showing identification.

Of course, if it didn't work, I could end up in 'deep doo-doo,' to use one of Kimo's favorite terms. Buttaree's name was all over the local news and the employee might recognize it, realize I was trying to scam my way into her locker, and call the police. I'm pretty sure that wouldn't be a good look for someone who was already facing a murder charge, especially if the locker contained the stolen money. The cops would probably conclude that Buttaree and I were partners and I killed her because I didn't want to share the loot.

So, cancel that. Any plan that ended with me explaining my actions to the police was a definite no-no. I took a couple of hits off the joint and sat back to consider what else I could do to get into Buttaree's locker. Maybe a robbery? Just before closing time? But I didn't own a gun. So ... using what? My finger as a gun?

Yeah, right. That idea was worse than the one where I bribed an employee. And I knew, deep inside, that I didn't have the guts to commit a robbery. As I told Buttaree, back when I first met her, I'm a nice guy. I could never rob a place. So cancel that plan, too.

I was still trying to figure things out when my phone rang at about 8:40. Usually, a call coming in at that time of day would find me still asleep and would go to voicemail, but today – like many of my recent days – was unusual. I answered without looking to see who was calling.

"Hi, sweetie," said a feminine voice.

Only one person in the entire world calls me 'sweetie.' "Hey, Mom. Howzit?"

"I'm surprised you're awake."

"Yeah. I woke up and couldn't get back to sleep, so I got up."

"Because you're worried, right?"

"I guess."

"Try not to worry, Archie."

Easier said than done, I thought. "Okay, Mom. I'll try. Where are you? At the store?"

"Uh-huh. I'm just opening up."

"Where's dad? Ala Wai?"

"No. He went over to Kaneohe with some friends. They're gonna play at Pali today."

Pali Golf Course was a hilly, challenging, public course on the windward side of the island, completely different than Ala Wai, where my dad usually played. Ala Wai Golf Course just might be the flattest golf course in the world!

"He's gonna be in a bad mood when he comes home," I said, adding a little chuckle at the end.

"I know. He always is when they play somewhere else."

"Well, tell him I said hi." I seldom spoke directly with my dad – any information that flowed back and forth between us usually was passed along by my mom. And that was because conversations with my dad inevitably ended up with him telling me to 'either go back to school and get your degree or get a real job!' and with me being pissed off.

"So, do you need some help?"

"Help?"

"You know, like money. For a lawyer."

"You've been talking to Pops, haven't you?"

"Yeah, he told me about what's happening. He said you're probably gonna be arrested for killing that girl, Buttaree."

"I didn't do it, Mom."

"I know, sweetie. I know you couldn't do something like that."

"And I'm fine. I don't need any money." At least, not yet, I thought.

"Okay. But if you do, you know you can count on us."

"Thanks, Mom. But I'm okay, really. And if I do need help, well, I'll ask you for it."

"Good. Don't be shy."

"I won't."

"I have to open up the store now. So ... call me. Keep me up to date with what's going on."

"I will."

"'Bye, sweetie. Love ya."

"I love you, too, Mom. Goodbye." I hung up.

And another awkward conversation with my mother comes to a close! It's always struck me as strange that I can have perfectly normal, pleasant, in-person conversations with my mom but put us on the phone with each other and things always seem uncomfortable. Especially when it's time to say goodbye.

Anyway, it was past nine – time to check out Kozy Keeps Mini-Storage. I pulled up Google once again to make sure I knew where to go, although I don't know why. I grew up in this area and I know my way around the Kapahulu and Kaimuki neighborhoods almost as well as I know my way around my apartment. And one thing I knew was that there was unlikely to be parking anywhere close to Kozy Keeps.

Not a problem. It was a beautiful morning, perfect for a walk. It couldn't be much more than 15 minutes away from here and I definitely could use the exercise. I spent entirely too much time sitting on this couch, smoking weed and drinking beer, and it was beginning to show on my waistline.

I dragged my lazy ass off the couch, changed my clothes, turned off the coffee, and headed out to find Kozy Keeps. Although I still hadn't figured out a way to get into Buttaree's locker, I wasn't too concerned about that. When I needed it, a plan of action would present itself, I felt sure. In the meantime, I just wanted to see what the place looked like.

It was a little after nine when I left. As I left the building and started up the street toward Ala Wai Boulevard, I noticed a black sedan, parked down the street near Kuhio Avenue. Although I'm not sure why, it struck me as suspicious. It might have been because it was so clean and shiny that it stood out from other cars in the neighborhood, most of which were covered with the daily dust and grime that comes with city life.

Whatevahs. It was freaking me out a bit. My imagination began to get involved. It's probably the cops, keeping an eye on you, it told me. Or maybe not – maybe it's those two 'detectives' from L.A. and they know I found the key and that I'm heading to Kozy Keeps and they intend to follow me and ... and ... do something, I just don't know what. Maybe try to steal the key from me?

Oh, stop! said that little voice inside my head. *You're being paranoid. It's only a car. A nice, shiny, black car.*

Got it. Only a car. But, just to be on the safe side, I deliberately dropped my keys on the sidewalk, took a couple of steps and then, pretending to realize what had happened, I turned back to pick them up. As I bent down to get my keys, I sneaked in a quick peek at that shiny black car.

If I tried really hard, I could just barely convince myself two men were sitting in the front seat, watching me walk up the street. In reality, though, I couldn't see into the car. All I could see was a giant reflection of the sun bouncing off the windshield, hiding whoever was inside. That is, if anyone *was* inside.

I retrieved my keys and continued up the street toward Ala Wai Boulevard. However, when I got to the corner, instead of turning right, which would lead me over to Kapahulu Avenue and Kozy Keeps Mini-Storage, I turned to my left. As I walked down Ala Wai to the next block and turned on Ohua Avenue, I hatched a plan to see if that shiny black car would follow me.

It was simple, really. All three of these streets – Paoakalani, Ala Wai, and Ohua – are one-way streets. Paoakalani leads up to Ala Wai, where you have to turn left, and Ohua leads back down to Kuhio Avenue. My plan was to walk completely around the block, ending back at my place, and see if the shiny black car followed me. Of course, when you're walking, it doesn't make any difference in which direction you go, but if anyone wanted to follow me in a car, I was making it super easy for them.

However, frequent glances behind me revealed no cars – shiny or otherwise – surreptitiously shadowing me as I walked down Ohua toward Kuhio Avenue. I didn't know whether to be disappointed or relieved. *Paranoia reigns supreme*, commented the little voice in my head.

I turned left on Kuhio and arrived at the corner of Paoakalani just in time to see to see the black shiny car pull out, go up the street and disappear around the corner onto Ala Wai Boulevard. If they were trying to follow me, they weren't doing a very good job, I decided. Still, as I headed up the street, anxiety over my plan to visit Kozy Keeps was building and that little voice inside me seemed to have switched sides and was now reinforcing my paranoia, telling me, *They're watching you. Someone's watching you.* So instead of continuing all the way up to Ala Wai Boulevard, when I came to my apartment building, I turned and went back in. It had been a nice 5-minute walk around the block. My trip to Kozy Keeps could wait until later.

Chapter Twenty-One

Thursday

The rest of Wednesday was lost in a fog of anxiety, beer, and pakalolo smoke – I never did make it to Kozy Keeps. I went to bed late Wednesday evening and awoke Thursday morning with a medium-strength hangover. Nevertheless, I struggled out of bed, made some coffee, and sat on my couch, drinking it, until I felt almost normal. By that time it was almost noon.

Yesterday's plan – the trip to Kozy Keeps – was also the plan for today. But first I needed to get something to eat. I got dressed and headed for Kapahulu Avenue, this time by way of Kuhio. No suspicious-looking cars lurked in the neighborhood or followed me as I made my way over to one of my favorite hamburger joints, Bobo's Big Bad Burgers. At least, as far as I could tell.

A couple of Bobo's famous Maui onion burgers and a Coke later, I was onion-burping my way up Kapahulu, heading for Kozy Keeps. I've always loved onions but it's an unrequited love – they return my love with a slightly upset stomach and nasty, burning burps. Still, in my opinion it's a worthwhile trade-off. I popped an antacid into my mouth, which usually calms things down somewhat.

As I proceeded up Kapahulu, past Ala Wai Boulevard, the canal and the golf course, it was a beautiful early-autumn day. The temperature was somewhere in the mid-eighties, the sun was shining brightly in a sky filled with a few small, puffy clouds, and a gentle breeze blew down over the Ko'olau Mountains, making it feel cool and warm at the same time. It was the type of day tourists pay big bucks to experience.

For me, though, the beauty and tranquility of the day went practically unnoticed as each step I took brought with it an increasing amount of anxiety. It wasn't an emotion that was strange to me, but it was one that, despite my current problems with the police, hadn't been around to any great degree recently – since before I met Buttaree, actually. I was beginning to understand what she was feeling, back when she was being followed by Thomas Mangrum.

By the time I crossed Date Street, my anxiety had morphed into paranoia. Every third car that went by seemed to be shiny and black and looked as if it contained undercover police. Or perhaps those were mobsters from the mainland, keeping an eye on me to see what I was up to. I was blanketed by this feeling that everyone around me knew what my plans were and I was just seconds away from being surrounded by 35 cops, all asking me the same question – Just what do you think you're doing, Mr. Morris?

Yeah. Just what did I think I was doing, anyway? What was the plan? What was I going to do, once I got to Kozy Keeps? How was I going to get into Buttaree's locker to see what was in it? I had plenty of questions but no answers, and that was making me extremely nervous.

My anxiety got to a point where I wasn't sure I could continue. I stopped briefly and took several deep breaths, hoping they would have a calming effect. And they did – up to a point. I felt a little bit better. So, in spite of my lack of a plan and the feelings of impending doom constantly threatening me, I continued my trek up Kapahulu, taking an occasional deep breath and blowing it out slowly as I walked along.

The deep breaths seemed to help but as I passed Winam Avenue, I caught a glimpse of a small sign up ahead – Kozy Keeps Mini-Storage – and the cloud of anxiety and paranoia that had been following me swooped down, enveloped me and wouldn't leave. Suddenly, everyone around me on the crowded sidewalk knew who I was and what I was up to, and they all were staring at me. At least, that's how it felt. I took several rapid deep breaths – hyperventilating, really – and walked right on past Kozy Keeps, never even looking at the place. *Chicken!* cried the little voice in my head. I ignored it and kept walking.

As I got past Kozy Keeps, the paranoia I'd been feeling began to diminish slightly, aided by a few more deep breaths. I came across a small coffee shop, went in and got a coffee and a sweet roll to go, ignoring the odd looks coming from the teenage girl behind the counter. Those looks were real – not a product of my imagination – but I doubted she knew who I was or what my plans were. She was probably wondering why I was all sweaty and why my hands were shaking. I felt as if I should explain my situation to her – tell her about the hot noonday sun and lie about how I had low blood sugar – but I knew her interest in my story was hovering right around zero percent so I kept my mouth shut, paid the bill and left.

Farther up the street, where Kapahulu intersects with Kaimuki Avenue, is an entrance to Crane Park, a small neighborhood park with benches beneath shady trees, a couple of basketball courts, and a large field where kids play football, baseball and softball. On the other side of that field is Kaimuki High School, where once upon a time Kimo was a star athlete and I was ... well, I was Kimo's friend. Anyway, my point is, having gone to high school just a few hundred yards away, I'm pretty familiar with this area.

I took my coffee and sweet roll into the park and sat on one of the concrete benches. An older haole woman, sitting on a bench across from me, watched as I sat down, so I nodded and smiled at her. She immediately closed the book she was reading, got up and left the park, heading up toward the freeway and Kaimuki town. That seemed a bit odd. Was I really that scary-looking?

Whatevahs. I sat and ate my snack while I considered what had just happened. With the Kozy Keeps caper, I mean. The more I thought about it, the more I convinced myself that I'd done the right thing by walking past the store without paying any special attention to it. That way, if anyone was following me or somehow watching me, they'd think I was just out for a walk on a nice day, maybe trying to get a little exercise. And now I was rewarding myself with a snack.

Some young kids were playing basketball on one of the two courts, while an older guy practiced his free throw shooting on the other. I watched them for a while while I ate, vaguely wondering why the kids weren't in school. Perhaps it was too nice a day for school and they were taking a 'sunshine day,' something I'd done a couple of times when I was their age.

Actually, it wasn't the kids that occupied my real interest – it was my surroundings. From where I was sitting I could see both Kaimuki Avenue and Kapahulu Avenue where they intersected. I could also see the sidewalks on both sides of those streets and far up Kapahulu, almost to the freeway. Hopefully, I'd be able to see anyone who might be following me, either on foot or in a black shiny car. Or in any kind of car, for that matter. However, in spite of my vigilance, I didn't see anyone or anything that looked suspicious.

That doesn't mean we aren't being followed, said the little voice in my head. *You could just be lousy at spotting someone tailing us.*

The little voice had a point, I decided. For today, it might be best if I didn't visit the Kozy Keeps store. That way, if anyone was following me, nothing I was doing would seem out of the ordinary in any way – I'd be just a regular guy taking a walk on a nice day. I tossed my trash in the can conveniently located at the end of my bench and headed back down Kapahulu toward Waikiki.

This time, knowing I didn't intend to stop, there was very little anxiety as I approached Kozy Keeps. I even glanced in the window as I walked past. There wasn't much to see, though – a counter with a clerk behind it, a couple of doors off to one side, and a huge sign on the wall that read, NOT RESPONSIBLE FOR LOST OR STOLEN ITEMS.

I can handle this, I told myself as I walked by. It won't be that difficult. I'll think of a plan to get into Buttaree's locker and then I'll do it. But not today. Maybe tomorrow.

Sure, said my little voice. *Tomorrow's good.*

Chapter Twenty-Two

Friday

Friday turned out to be a repeat of Thursday, just without the hangover. At least, the first part of it. I woke up in a bit of a funk, got up, made coffee and sat on my couch, drinking it and watching various shows while I tried to come up with some method of accessing Kozy Keeps locker number 31.

A couple of joints occasionally called to me from my coffee table, but I knew smoking weed intensified my feelings of anxiety and paranoia so I ignored them, even when they tried to convince me they were really just appetite medicine. A clear head was what I needed, not a buzz, in order to come up with a plan. Also, when I get stoned, I don't really get a lot done.

By noon, though, I hadn't come up with any cool or sneaky methods of conning my way into Buttaree's locker, so I got dressed and headed out to get some lunch. I walked down past Kuhio Avenue and Cartwright Road and turned left on Lemon Road, which led me directly over to Kapahulu Avenue and my favorite lunchwagon, Pua's Plenny Big Kine Plate Lunch. Then, a teriyaki chicken plate with extra rice and macaroni salad in hand, I wandered into Kapiolani Park, grabbed a spot beneath a huge banyan tree and sat down to eat.

My original plan was to eat and then head back up Kapahulu to Kozy Keeps, repeating my trip of the day before but hopefully without the anxiety and paranoia. However, as I sat there in the cool shade of the tree, eating my lunch, I realized my project for the day was still lacking one major ingredient – the how factor. How, exactly, was I going to get into Buttaree's locker? Without having the answer to that question, there didn't seem to be much point to the rest of the plan. I'd probably just pull a repeat of yesterday – getting paranoid and walking right on past the place, accomplishing nothing.

I decided to go home and think about it some more. Which I did, walking along Kalakaua toward the heart of Waikiki until I came to Paoakalani, only a block away from Kapahulu down at this end, near the beach, and then up the three short blocks to my apartment building. And by the time I was back in my apartment, I'd come up with a new plan.

Unfortunately, my new plan had nothing to do with getting into Buttaree's locker. In fact, it seemed like more of an excuse not to do that because there were other things – important things – I needed to do. And even though those other, important things actually consisted of just a couple of phone calls, that was enough justification for me to postpone the day's planned trip to Kozy Keeps Mini-Storage.

Sure, said my little voice, agreeing with me once again. *No big hurry.*

Once I was again comfortably ensconced on my couch, I made the first of those calls – to my boss. My current schedule was perhaps best described as 'on hold,' but I felt as if I needed still more time off. I decided to tell him I was suffering from PTSD – Post Traumatic Stress Disorder.

He was pretty understanding about it – at first. But then he started telling me about how business had been slow lately and how he was afraid he might even be losing money instead of making it and suddenly I found myself suffering from an entirely different affliction, PESD – Post Employment Stress Disorder. He fired me.

Actually, the amount of stress the firing generated was minimal. I hated the job – the hours, the pay, the lack of benefits, everything about it – and was glad to be done with it. But it did mean I was going to have to start looking for a new job sooner than I'd intended and that, of course, was never much fun.

Try to see the bright side, was my little voice's advice. *Now you'll have more time to figure out how to break into Kozy Keeps.*

I wanted to correct my little voice's use of the the expression *break in* to describe what I intended to do, but I knew that would just result in me arguing with myself, and that was an argument I couldn't win. Besides, he could be right – if I couldn't come up with a good plan, maybe breaking into the place was the only answer.

Of course, I doubted I could actually do that. Heck, I couldn't even walk past the place without suffering a panic attack. The chances I'd be able to commit a burglary were somewhere between zero and none.

Keep an open mind, my little voice said. *You never know what you're capable of until you actually try it.*

My little voice was wrong this time, I was certain. There was absolutely, positively no way I could turn myself into a burglar. I just wasn't the type.

A call to Detective Higa was next on my afternoon agenda. But as I started to make the call, a slight problem arose – I didn't have his number. I remembered that he'd given me a business card with his cell phone number on it, but I couldn't remember what I'd done with the card.

No need to panic, I told myself. Just call the police station, ask to speak to Detective Higa and they'll connect you. Simple.

But that, of course, seemed like way too easy a solution. I needed more of a challenge, so the next 20 minutes were spent searching my apartment for the missing card. It turned up hiding between a couple of couch cushions, and I sat back down to call Detective Higa.

"Amos Higa," he answered.

"Hello?" I replied. Suddenly, this felt like a bad idea and I wasn't sure how I was going to broach the subject of whether or not I was being followed.

Good time to think of that, now, chipped in my always-helpful little friend.

"How are you holding up, Mr. Morris?"

"It's Archie," I reminded him. Since there had never been any phone communications between us, I was surprised he recognized my number.

"Right. So, how are you doing, Archie?"

"Okay, I guess."

"What can I do for you today?"

"Uh, I hear you're off my case, that you've handed your findings over to the District Attorney's office. Is that true?"

A long pause followed. Finally, Detective Higa said, "Sorry. I was distracted for a moment. As for your question, the answer is a sort-of yes."

"Sort of? What's that mean?"

"It means that my investigation is over and I've turned the results over to the D.A. But we're still waiting on information from a connected, ongoing investigation in California. In Los Angeles. When that comes in, we'll turn that over, also, and the investigative part of the case will be over."

"Los Angeles? What's going on there?"

"I'm sorry, Archie. I'm not really at liberty to discuss that."

"Oh. Yeah, of course. Anyway, that's not why I called."

"No? What do you need?"

"You're not having me followed, are you?"

"Followed?" Detective Higa chuckled. "I'm pretty sure we're not doing that."

"Really?"

"Yes, really, Archie. We don't have enough officers or enough money to follow suspects around. But we do have officers stationed at the airport to keep an eye out for those we think might try to leave the island."

I couldn't think of any intelligent reply to that so I said, "Oh," and let it go at that.

"Why? Were you thinking of running away?"

It was my turn to chuckle. "No, I wasn't. It's just that, well, I went for a walk yesterday, and there was this suspicious car and … ah, it's probably nothing. Just paranoia on my part."

"I can assure you it wasn't us. We just can't afford to do that. Do you want me to check it out for you?"

"Check it out? How can you do that? It happened yesterday."

"Cameras, Archie. Cameras," Detective Higa said, and I could almost hear the smile on his face as he said it. "Cameras are everywhere these days."

"No, there's no need to check it out. Like I said, it's probably nothing."

"All right, then. Anything else?"

"I don't suppose you can tell me anything about the case. About your recommendations, I mean."

"I'm sorry, I can't. And recommendations aren't involved, Archie. I just turn the results of my investigation over to the D.A.'s office and they decide what to do with it."

"Yeah, of course. Okay, then. That's it. I'm sorry to have bothered you," I said.

"Not a problem," Detective Higa said, and hung up.

With my plans for the day – excluding the now-canceled trip back to Kozy Keeps – successfully concluded, I got a beer from the fridge and sat back to consider what Detective Higa had told me. Evidently, all I could do was wait to see what the District Attorney's office had in store for me. I was either going to be indicted for murder or not. It was a distinctly unpleasant feeling knowing my future was entirely in the hands of someone else and there wasn't anything I could do about it.

Chapter Twenty-Three

Saturday

Kimo showed up early on Saturday, bringing beer, assorted pupus, and good news.

"Good news?" I said, putting things away in the kitchen. "I could use some of that." I grabbed a couple of beers and joined him on my couch.

"Are you ready for this?" he said. "Maybe you'd better sit down."

"I am sitting down, dummy."

He looked at me and a sheepish grin spread across his face. "Oh. Okay. Anyway, you won't believe the story I'm gonna tell you."

"Yeah?"

"Yeah."

"About what?"

"About your friend, Buttaree."

"What about her?"

"You're not gonna believe me," Kimo repeated. He was practically giddy with excitement and I could tell he was dying to tell me what it was.

I feigned indifference. "Yeah, you better not tell me, then, if I'm not gonna believe it."

"You're off the hook!" he practically shouted at me.

"What? What are you talking about?"

"Buttaree's murder. You're off the hook for it. They're not gonna indict you."

"Really?"

"Really."

"That's great." I've often heard of people in situations like this – finding out some piece of news that brings them immediate relief from a stressful predicament – describing it as having 'a huge weight lifted from them,' and I always thought that was an exaggeration. But, to tell you the truth, that's exactly how I felt. Suddenly lighter. Much lighter.

"That's it? You find out you're not going to go to jail for the rest of your life and all you can say is, 'That's great?'"

"What do you want me to say?"

"I dunno. But if it was me I'd be dancing a little jig, maybe doing cartwheels or something."

I laughed. "I'd like to see that."

"Actually, so would I," he said, laughing with me.

"So how do you know they don't plan to indict me?" I said, and then, with hardly a pause, I answered my own question. "Oh, Pops."

"Yeah, Pops was at the station this morning and they told him about it."

"So ... how come? They got another suspect?"

Kimo took a swig of his beer and shook his head. "They got some info from the Los Angeles police. And this is the part that's unbelievable."

"Just tell me, already."

"Well, that detective who was handling your case – Higa – got the report from the cops in L.A. And this case just blew up into something major. For one thing, your friend, Buttaree – that's not her real name."

"What?"

"Her name's not Buttaree Gudnis. Well, it is, but it isn't."

"Make up your mind." I lit a joint and passed it over to Kimo.

"You smoke too much," he said, taking a big hit.

"That's because my best friend gave me a lifetime supply of weed."

"Not gonna last a lifetime, the way you smoke it." He took another hit and passed the joint back to me.

"So if her name's not Buttaree Gudnis, what is it?" I said.

"You ready for this?" He leaned forward and used his fingers to perform a drum roll on my coffee table. "Ta-dah! It's ... Penelope Sux."

"What?!!"

"She's a porn star named Penelope Sux. Or, she was a porn star. Pretty big, too, supposedly."

"You're kidding!"

"Nope. It's the truth. Your buddy, Buttaree, was actually a porn actor called Penelope Sux."

"This is unbelievable," I said.

"I told you that."

"Yeah, you did. So, what does that have to do with me? The fact that her real name was ... what?"

"Buttaree Gudnis. That was her real name. And Penelope Sux was her porn name," Kimo said.

"Good name for a porn star, I guess. But it still doesn't explain why they're not going to indict me."

"Oh, that's just the beginning of the story. There's lots more."

"So tell me, already."

"You know that guy, Harry Dick, who hired Mangrum to look for Buttaree?"

"Richard something."

"Harrodi. Richard Harrodi. He's a porn producer. He owns a company called Harry Dick Productions. And Buttaree worked for him, performing under the name Penelope Sux."

"Okay, I got that part." To tell the truth, I was having a hard time accepting the fact that the sweet, friendly girl I knew was a porno actor, but I knew Kimo wouldn't lie to me about something this important. It had to be true.

"So, this is what the L.A. police think happened. Buttaree wanted to quit, to get out of the business. So she sets up a meeting with her producer, Harrodi, to discuss what she needs to do to get out of her contract. The meeting's in the early evening and when she shows up at his office, she finds him passed out at his desk."

I nodded to let Kimo know I was keeping up with his story.

"There's a half-empty bottle of whiskey on his desk and a small suitcase sitting on the floor next to it. The cops think Buttaree saw the suitcase, got curious and opened it, and found it was full of money. So she took it and split to Hawaii."

"How much money? Do they know?"

"Not for sure. But if it was so much that he had to put it in a suitcase, it must have been a lot."

"Wow," was all I could think of to say.

"Yeah, wow, all right. Anyway, supposedly this guy, Harrodi, was mobbed up, and the money in the suitcase was sitting there, waiting to be picked up by some low-level mob guy and delivered to a guy named Tommy Sarfeen. T-Bag, they call him. This guy, Sarfeen, describes himself as an 'angel investor,' but he's actually a loan shark and he's also the brains and money behind Harry Dick Productions."

"This is getting kinda complicated."

"Yeah, just wait. It gets worse."

"Okay, so then what?"

"Well, with the money missing, Harrodi is in big trouble with the mob, but he figures out pretty quickly who took it because both the money and Buttaree disappeared at the same time. He also gets a tip she came here, to Hawaii, so he hires that private eye, Mangrum, to find her."

"Which he did."

"Right. So then Harrodi sends a couple of mob goons over here to get his money back from Buttaree."

"Oh, the 'detectives' in the shiny suits that took over from Mangrum."

"Yeah, those guys. So now they're number one on the cops' list, not you. The theory is they were torturing Buttaree by dunking her under the water, trying to get her to tell them where she hid the money, and they accidentally drowned her. At least, that's one of the theories."

A sense of vindication swept over me. This was the same theory I'd been promoting in an effort to save myself from a lengthy prison sentence. I was right all along!

"So, a couple of interesting sidebars to all this," Kimo continued. "The cops in L.A. can't find Harrodi – he's missing. And the local cops can't find the two guys from the mainland. They're missing, too."

"What's that mean? They're in hiding?"

"Either that or the mob got rid of them."

"What about the money?"

"Still missing, as far as anyone knows."

"No one knows what happened to it?"

"Nope. They're not even a hundred percent sure Buttaree was the one who took it, but that's the best working theory. The whole thing is just one big puzzle right now. But, like I said, it gets you off the hook."

I leaned forward, lit up a fresh joint and passed it over to Kimo. "It's a puzzler, huh? So what's the official conclusion on all this?"

"There isn't one. Half the cops think the two goons found the money and decided to keep it. That they didn't accidentally kill Buttaree before she could tell them where she hid it, they killed her after she told them. Then they collected the money and disappeared. The cops are checking on flights out of here right after Buttaree got killed, but so far they haven't found anything."

"You said half the cops believe that's what happened. What about the other half? What do they think?"

"That the money's still around, somewhere, but nobody knows where. Only Buttaree knew and she died before she told anyone. The two goons accidentally drowned her before she could talk." He took a big hit and passed the joint back to me. "Unless she told you," he said, exhaling.

I looked at him. He seemed serious. "Me? Why would she tell me where she'd stashed a bunch of money?" I took a hit and put the joint in the ashtray.

"Well, you were her friend. Like, her only friend here in town, as far as anyone knows."

"Right. So the porn star with a heart of gold just happened to let me in on her little secret – where she hid her stolen loot – 'cause I'm such a good friend."

"Well, when you put it like that, it does sound kinda stupid. Anyway, I think the two goons got it."

"Yeah, that's what happened. Probably." I felt a little guilty, lying to Kimo, but there wasn't any good reason to bring up my finding a key to a locker that might – just might – hold the missing money. I'd make the decision on whether or not to tell Kimo about that once I knew for sure what the locker contained. After all, that might not be where the money is. In fact, Buttaree's locker might even be empty, in which case I'd be extremely disappointed.

We spent the rest of the afternoon drinking beer and watching a rerun of a three-year-old football game. Kimo seemed to get into the game – Notre Dame, a team we both hated, was beating some little college by 33 points – but my head was full of other things and I basically just stared at the screen while my thoughts were far away. Based on this new information, I was pretty sure that if Buttaree did take the money – which seemed likely – she'd stashed it in locker number 31 at Kozy Keeps Mini-Storage. Now all I had to do was figure out a way to get it.

Chapter Twenty-Four

Saturday/Sunday

Kimo left at about seven to get ready for a date with his new main squeeze, Kelly. I stayed on the couch, drinking and smoking and trying to come up with a trouble-free way to find out what was in locker 31. By 2 AM, though, no easy plan had presented itself so I went to bed.

After tossing and turning for what seemed like hours, I finally fell asleep. Although I'm not usually much of a dreamer – most nights I have absolutely no sense of dreaming – this night was different. I was presented with a strange scenario, full of bizarre characters and surreal situations. Actually, in that sense, I guess it was pretty much like most dreams – weird.

Anyway, Buttaree was in it and she seemed to be the star. She was walking up Kapahulu Avenue, totally naked, carrying a medium-size overnight bag that was overflowing with cash. The bag was so stuffed that bills were falling out as she walked along and a group of people were following her, picking up money as it fell to the pavement. She seemed oblivious both to the fact that she was losing money and that she was being followed, and also that she was the only one who was naked.

Some of the characters in the group following her looked vaguely familiar. At the front of the pack was at least one easily-recognized evil character – Snidely Whiplash, a villain from the old Rocky and Bullwinkle animated TV show, complete with extra-long, handlebar mustache and leering grin. He was engaged in what appeared to be a three-way sumo match for control of the fallen money with two people I couldn't quite identify, although one of them looked vaguely like Mrs. Nakamura, my third-grade teacher. But there really was no need to push and shove, as Buttaree's overnight bag seemed to have an inexhaustible supply of cash streaming from it and there appeared to be plenty for everybody.

At the back of the trailing crowd, I followed, desperately – and unsuccessfully – trying to break through, to warn her she was in danger. It was no use, though. Over and over, I'd back up and rush the crowd, only to be rebuffed. It was getting tiring.

Eventually, I became so tired I had to stop and rest. I stood there, hands on knees, panting for breath, watching as Buttaree and the crowd continued up Kapahulu without me. Across the street, a truck pulled out of Rainbow Drive-In, drove over to where I was standing and began backing up, toward me, on the sidewalk. I could hear it's back-up warning signal – beep, beep, beep – but when I tried to get out of the way, my legs refused to cooperate. I was rooted to the sidewalk, unable to move.

Beep, beep beep. The truck – a big step-van – was only a couple of feet away and seemed destined to back right over me. Still without the ability to move my feet, I raised both hands and prepared to give the truck a big whack just before it hit me. Maybe the driver would hear it and stop in time to prevent me from being flattened against the sidewalk.

BEEP! BEEP! BEEP! Only inches separated me from my impending doom. I braced myself for impact. And then ... I sat up, awake. There was no truck. My alarm clock, which was permanently set for 11 o'clock to prevent me from oversleeping, was beeping. I reached out and turned it off.

I was soaking wet with sweat, as were my sheets, which clung to me like the cold embrace of a corpse. Shivering, I got up and started my day by stripping my bed and taking a shower. As I said, I'm not much of a dreamer, but a day of drinking beer and smoking weed will give you a strange dream or two, I guess.

Perhaps it meant something. The dream, I mean. Maybe it was a message from Buttaree, sent from the Great Beyond. There are people who believe in things like that – dreams having meanings and secret messages sent from, ... from, ... well, I don't know where they come from, but I do know they're purposely confusing and difficult to figure out.

I've never been one of those people – dream interpreters, or whatever you call them. That's probably because I don't dream much and never have, so there's never been much to interpret. But last night's dream intrigued me. I sat on the couch with my usual breakfast – coffee and a joint – and tried to figure out what it meant, if anything.

Was it possible it had been a message? From Buttaree? A warning? About what? People following me, maybe? Or perhaps, watch out for trucks that are backing up? Who knew what any of it meant? I was unable to come up with anything that made sense.

There was, of course, an obvious explanation for what I was doing, sitting on my couch trying to figure out my nonsensical dream. I was deliberately stalling, delaying my big plan for the day – another trip up Kapahulu to Kozy Keeps. I'd more or less promised myself that I'd give that trip another try, maybe stop and look in the window, maybe even go inside and get some information, if I felt calm enough. Although that last part was beginning to seem more and more unlikely, as a growing sense of apprehension had already descended upon me. It wasn't yet full-blown anxiety but it was certainly a good beginning.

It was at about this time that my little voice made his first appearance of the day. *I can't believe you're so stupid*, he said.

And good morning to you, too. But don't you mean we? We're so stupid?

No, I mean you. After all, I'm the one who has a plan.

You have a plan?

I do.

What is it? Tell me.

It's simple, actually.

So tell me. What is it?

How to get into Buttaree's locker.

Really? How?

Rent your own locker!

Pow! Just like that, all parts of the plan – the Kozy Keeps Plan, as I'd come to think of it – fell into place. I couldn't believe the answer was so simple. Rent a locker. And then what?

Play it by ear, came the suggestion. *Get inside, take a look around, and then we can make a plan that works.*

Your plan sounds like half a plan – a plan to make a plan.

Whatevahs. Half a plan is better than no plan at all.

I wasn't sure I completely agreed with that assessment. 'Half a plan' might just be another way of saying 'half-assed plan,' and a half-assed plan was more likely to get me arrested than to get me into Buttaree's locker. Still, I hadn't come up with anything better, so maybe it was worth a shot.

Chapter Twenty-Five

I finished my coffee and smoke and left about two o'clock, walking down to Kuhio and then over to Kapahulu. Since Paoakalani, the street I live on, was one-way in the opposite direction – toward Ala Wai Boulevard – I figured that would make it difficult for anyone to follow me in a car. Some would consider that to be evidence of paranoia, I suppose, but to me it seemed like a reasonable precaution for someone in my position. However, no suspicious-looking vehicles appeared to be following me.

As I started up Kapahulu, the anxiety I'd felt during my previous trip returned, but to a much smaller degree. I took a few deep breaths and tried to talk myself into a calmer state, reminding myself I was 'just out for a walk on a nice day.' And it was a nice day. Beautiful, actually. The trade winds were gently blowing, the sun shone brightly in a sky nearly devoid of clouds, and off to my right, Diamond Head stood sway over Waikiki and the surrounding area. All seemed right with the world.

Kapahulu Avenue hadn't changed much since I was a kid. Some things were different, of course. Older stores and coffee shops were gone, replaced by newer ones that sold much the same things, but the mainstays of my youth – Rainbow Drive-In, Zippy's, the bank where I had my first savings account – were still around. And as I passed Winam Avenue, I could see Leonard's Bakery, home of those delicious, donut-like, sugar-coated, light-as-air Portuguese pastries called *malasadas,* up ahead on the right, across from Crane Park. It had been years since I'd had a malasada – not since I was in high school. They used to give you 13 of them if you ordered a dozen. I wondered if they still did that.

My emotional state was definitely better than on my previous trip but, as I got closer to Kozy Keeps, that old, familiar, anxious feeling began to return, and when I came upon the place, I walked on by without so much as a sideways glance.

I thought we were going to stop, look in the window, maybe even go inside and ask some questions, piped up my little voice.

That's what I thought, too.

So what happened?

I'm not ready. I need to build up my courage.

You need courage for that? To look in a window?

I wanna go inside and look around.

Okay. That sounds good.

But ...

What?

I'm hungry. I need to eat something.

That's just an excuse.

No, I'm really hungry. Let's get something to eat, then I'll check out Kozy Keeps.

Promise?

Uh, ... sure.

You're such a wuss! Was that my little voice or was it me? It didn't make much difference. Either way, the diagnosis was correct, and I knew it. I was a wuss!

Farther up the sidewalk, the coffee shop at which I'd previously bought coffee beckoned me, so I went in. After checking out the various pastries, I decided I wasn't really that hungry and settled for a coffee to go. Then I headed up the street to Crane Park, where, once again, I ended up sitting on a concrete bench, drinking coffee while trying to work up enough courage to go check out Kozy Keeps.

This is ridiculous. My little voice always was good at stating the obvious.

I can't help it. It's my P.P.D.

Oh, bull! Paranoid Personality Disorder? That's just some crap a shrink told you once and you've been using it as an excuse ever since.

No. It's true. I get anxious.

That's not a real excuse – everyone gets anxious when they have to do something out of the ordinary. Do what they do.

Which is?

Suck it up and act like a man!

I was saved from this endless argument with myself by the arrival of the older haole woman I'd seen in the park the previous Thursday. She walked in carrying a large hardcover book and took a seat on the bench opposite me. As I'd done the last time, I smiled and nodded at her. And, as she'd done the last time, she immediately got up to leave.

Except, this time she didn't leave. She walked over to me and said, "I know who you are."

Caught by surprise, all I could respond with was, "You do?"

"You're Meredith Morris."

Meredith? Nobody calls me Meredith. Even the newspaper identified me as Archibald 'Archie' Morris. I looked more carefully at her face. She looked vaguely familiar.

"You don't recognize me, do you?" she said.

"I'm afraid I don't."

"Mrs. Dansereau. I was the school librarian at Waikiki Elementary when you were a student there."

Oh, yeah. Mrs. Dansereau. Hilda the Dancer, we used to call her, although I have no idea why.

She continued, "I'm the one who caught you and your friend – that big Hawaiian boy – trying to steal books."

"Kimo. We weren't trying to steal them. I fact, he wasn't doing anything – it was only me. And I was just trying to borrow them but you wouldn't let me because I lost my library card."

"I consider that stealing."

"Whatevahs." I was surprised I hadn't recognized her, considering the fact she'd caused me so much grief back when I was in fifth grade. Heck, if it hadn't been for the intervention of Pops, I might have ended up being arrested, since the three books I dropped out the library window were worth a total of over $100, according to Mrs. Dansereau.

"Why aren't you in jail?" said Hilda the Dancer.

"In jail? For stealing – I mean, borrowing books? Almost 20 years ago?"

"For killing that girl, that stripper."

"Oh, that. I didn't kill her. They're looking for someone else."

"I always knew you'd end up no good, Meredith Morris. Any child who steals books is heading for a dim future, if you ask me."

This conversation was becoming tiring – I wasn't in the fifth grade anymore and I didn't have to listen to the school librarian haranguing me. I was a full-grown, almost-functioning adult. I smiled up at her. "No one asked you. And no one gives a crap what you think about any of this, least of all, me."

With a "harrumph," she turned and stomped out of the park.

"Nice seeing you again," I called after her, but if she heard me, she gave no indication of it. "And I hope I ruined your day," I added, more quietly, so that only my little voice and I heard it.

That went well, he said.

Oddly enough, I agreed. What appeared to have been an unpleasant encounter had actually cheered me up and I felt much better than I had just moments earlier. Most of the anxiety I'd been feeling had dissipated and a sense of calm had descended upon me. I knew what I had to do – investigate Kozy Keeps Mini-Storage – and I was ready to do it.

"Okay, buddy," I said out loud. "Let's go do this."

My little buddy remained silent, perhaps not trusting my resolution. Apparently, I was going to have to handle this on my own.

Chapter Twenty-Six

The clerk in Kozy Keeps looked at me suspiciously. Were beads of sweat popping out on my forehead, giving away my nefarious intentions? Damn! I sure hoped not. The last thing I needed was for some suspicious high school kid to report me to the cops. I'd be back at the top of the Buttaree-killer suspect list in record time.

"Basically, they're just square metal boxes and they come in three sizes, small, medium, and large," he was explaining to me. Small is two feet – eight cubic feet. Medium is three feet. That's 27 cubic feet. And our largest size is four feet, that's –"

"Let me guess. Sixty-four cubic feet?"

He grinned at me. "Right."

"What about the price?"

"It's 10, 17, and 25 bucks. Five bucks off if you pay for three months in advance."

"Can I take a look?"

"Sure. But there's not much to see." He pressed a button under the counter and one of the two doors against the back wall – the brown one – swung partly open with a soft groan. "They're just metal boxes that lock and at the end of the room there's some tables you can curtain off while you look at your stuff."

I followed him over to the open door and took a quick look inside the room. Basically, it was just as the kid had described – a bunch of square metal boxes and some tables. "All three sizes are in this room?"

"Yeah. The big ones are on the left and the other two sizes are on the right. And there's three tables."

"What's behind that other door? The green one."

"Oh, that's the bathroom. It's supposed to be only for employees but you can use it if you need to."

"No, I'm good. Just curious."

"You know, we recommend you don't store anything valuable here. Just personal items and stuff. You need to get a bank safe-deposit box for stashing jewelry and things like that." He pointed up at the NOT RESPONSIBLE FOR LOST OR STOLEN ITEMS sign on the wall behind the counter.

"No, nothing valuable. Some notebooks and personal papers. Nothing that important. I just need to get them out of my apartment – they're cluttering it up."

"Well, we're the place for that," the kid said cheerfully.

"Are they numbered?"

The kid looked confused. "What?"

"The lockers. Are they numbered?"

"Oh. Yeah, they are."

"You think I could get my lucky number?"

"Maybe. If it's not taken, already. I can look it up for you if you want. What is it?"

"Thirty-one."

We went back over to the counter and he tapped something into the tablet in front of him, but before he did, I thought I saw a look of surprise cross his face, a slight arching of the eyebrows when I told him my lucky number was 31. Of course, that might have been my imagination – just my normal paranoia poking up from my subconscious. But maybe not. It was remarkable how calm I felt, considering how long it had taken me to work up the courage to do this.

"I'm sorry," he said. "That locker's occupied."

"Damn."

"One of our other locations might have an open 31. I can check if you like."

"No, I live in Waikiki. I want something nearby."

He shook his head, grinned, and shrugged, all at the same time. "Sorry."

"What size is that, anyway? Number 31, I mean."

"It's a large."

"How about something close?" I said.

"Close?"

"Yeah, like number 30 or number 32 – close to 31."

"Oh, close. Sure. Lemme look." He checked his tablet. "Thirty's open."

"Is that a large?"

"Yup. And it's right next to 31. See?" He spun his tablet around for me to look at. A fairly self-explanatory diagram showed a block of squares, most of them with a large X inside. Thirty-one was Xed out, but right next to it, on the left, locker number 30 was blank.

"Okay. Gimme locker number 30, then."

"Great! I need an ID and a credit card." The kid was beaming, as if I'd just made his day. He probably got a commission for signing up new customers, was my guess.

I gave him my license and credit card, signed a couple of papers, and was presented with a small brass key, identical to the one already on my key ring except for the number.

"That's it," said the kid. "We're open from nine to nine. You can bring your stuff in anytime."

"When's a good time?"

"Good time? You can do it anytime."

"No, I mean, when is it crowded, not crowded? Like that."

"Oh. It's never really crowded. Probably early evening is when most people come in. But during the day and after, like, seven, it's like this."

Pretty slow." He waved his hand, indicating the store, empty except for the two of us.

"What do I do when I come in? Just show the key?"

"Yeah, usually that's all you need. When you're a new customer, like you, whoever's working might not recognize you and ask to see your ID before they buzz you into the back. But that's it."

"Okay, then. Thanks for your help."

"Not a problem. And welcome to the Kozy Keeps family, Mr. Morris."

From the embarrassed look on the kid's face, that must have been something he was required to say to new customers. I nodded, thanked him again and left. When I was outside, on the sidewalk, I took a couple of deep breaths and smiled. Mission accomplished! So far, so good!

That was easy, popped up my little voice. *Nothing to be afraid of.*

You're right, buddy. As usual.

We should have done this a long time ago.

Right, again.

So how come we didn't check out our new locker? Take a good look inside that room?

We'll get to that. Don't worry. One step at a time.

Yeah, one step at a time. And the next step was to go home and rest up for what would hopefully be the final step in my grand master plan – actually looking to see what was inside locker number 31.

I decided to take a different route home, not from any sense of anxiety or paranoia but from a sense of nostalgia. I walked back up to Crane Park and cut through it, across the basketball courts and the athletic field, and exited on the other side, on Olokele Avenue, right behind Kaimuki High School. When I was a teenager, this was the way I used to walk home from school – up Olokele to Date Street, up Date to Kapahulu, then up Campbell Avenue to Hinano Street and then Wela Street, the street where I lived. But if I was expecting this path to rekindle some feelings of teenage happiness and enthusiasm from my high school years – and I guess I was – I was disappointed. By the time I got to Kapahulu Avenue, I was feeling only one thing – hunger.

I crossed Kapahulu and went into Zippy's, a local restaurant popular for its good food and reasonable prices, and got myself a chili dog plate lunch with extra rice and macaroni salad. While I ate, I attempted to work out the remaining details of what both my little voice and I had apparently agreed to call 'the plan.'

The only thing I really needed was a container of some kind, and I was pretty sure that tucked away in the back of my clothes closet, untouched for years, was a gym bag that would easily fit into a four-by-four foot locker. All I had to do was stuff some old clothes into it to give it a bit of bulk and when I went back to Kozy Keeps, pretend it was the reason I'd needed to rent a locker. That way, everything I was doing would seem perfectly normal.

Unless we're being watched.

Watched?

By the cops.

Detective Higa said they weren't doing that.

And you believed him?

Yeah. I thought about that. Why should I believe what Detective Higa told me? He was a cop, after all. He seemed to be a nice guy but cops lie to suspects all the time, according to Pops. Cops can lie to you but you can't lie to them or it's a crime.

'Thanks a lot, buddy,' I said as I felt my anxiety start to return.

Not a problem. I'm here to help.

So walking up Kapahulu carrying a gym bag, on my way to Kozy Keeps, suddenly didn't seem like such a good idea. Of course, I could drive and probably find parking within a couple of blocks – maybe on Kaimuki Avenue, down the street from the park. But the cops – or anyone else who might be interested – could still follow me.

And then there was the matter of my car. I hadn't used it for weeks and the battery wasn't that strong. There was an excellent chance I'd need help to get it started.

The idea of taking a taxi or an Uber presented itself and was summarily dismissed. Too obvious. Me climbing into a taxi with a gym bag would surely set off alarm bells for anyone who was following me. So, with walking, driving, and taking a cab out of the question, I was left with the one option I probably should have started with – I needed Kimo to give me a ride and I needed him to be sneaky about it.

Chapter Twenty-Seven

Monday

The rest of Sunday and all of Monday morning was spent obsessed with the plan, going over it in my head and imagining possible outcomes. What would I find in Buttaree's locker, anyway? Would it be the missing money she'd supposedly stolen? If so, how much money would it be? Fifty thousand? Five million? Kimo and I had agreed that it had to be a significant amount or it wouldn't have been worth it to hire a private investigator and then send a couple of guys over here to retrieve it. I smiled inwardly as I imagined myself finding millions of dollars stashed away inside Kozy Keeps. I'd told the clerk my lucky number was 31 – perhaps it would turn out to be true.

Or maybe there would be no cash, just some old junk Buttaree didn't want cluttering up her apartment. But it didn't make much sense that she would have needed a locker to store junk – she'd told me once that because of the frequent relocating required by her job, she liked to travel light. I couldn't imagine her bringing a lot of useless crap with her from the mainland.

So it had to be the stolen money, I decided. And the only question was – how much? Just how rich was I going to be? What would I do with millions of dollars in tax-free cash, anyway? I leaned back and closed my eyes and let my thoughts wander. It was just after noon.

At around two, I woke up. I was starving. A cup of instant ramen solved that problem, and when I was finished eating, I lit up a joint and called Kimo.

"Wassup?" he answered.

"Hey, howzit? You busy?"

"Nope. Just sitting here wishing I was someplace else."

"Like at the beach, yeah?"

"Yeah."

"So how was your date with Kelly? You spend the weekend with
her?"

"The date was fine, but Sunday morning she went up to Makaha for
a couple of days. She'll be back tonight."

"What's in Makaha?"

"Her parents."

"Carl and ... ?"

"Jennifer. They belong to some private club up there and Kelly went
up to visit them. They're rich, you know."

"Really?"

"Yeah. Like, super-rich."

"That's good, I guess. Listen, I need a favor."

"Sure. What is it?"

That's one thing I've always liked about Kimo. Ask him for a favor
and he doesn't require advance information before giving you his
answer. None of that, 'Well, what is it?' or 'What do you want me to
do?' stuff before he gives you an answer. Just, 'sure.' In my mind, that
marks him as a true friend.

"I need a ride," I told him. "This evening."

"A ride? What's wrong with your car?"

"Nothing. I just don't wanna use it."

"Okay. Where to?"

"Leonard's Bakery."

There was a short pause on Kimo's end, then he laughed. "What?
You run out of malasadas?"

"Something like that. I don't want to explain it now – I'll tell you
later."

"All right. What time?"

"How's seven-thirty?"

"I can do that."

"Great. And don't tell anyone what you're doing. That you're giving me a ride, I mean. Especially Pops." It wasn't that I didn't trust Pops but, after all, he was once a cop. And I've heard it said, 'once a cop, always a cop.'

Another pause, this one quite a bit longer than the previous one, followed from Kimo. He probably considered that last request a little odd. Finally, he said, "This doesn't have anything to do with your friend, Buttaree, does it?"

"Like I said, I'll tell you all about it later."

"Okay. I'll pick you up at seven-thirty, then."

"One more thing."

"Yeah?"

"Pick me up on Ohua."

"Ohua?"

"You remember when the reporters were hanging around outside my place and we went out the back and cut over to Ohua?"

"Sure."

"That's what I'm gonna do. I don't want anyone to see me leave."

"How come? Someone watching your place?" Kimo said.

"Probably not, since it seems I'm not the number one suspect anymore. But I'm just being cautious. You know me. Always on the careful side."

"All right. I'll pick you up at seven-thirty. On Ohua."

"See you then."

I spent most of the rest of the afternoon sitting on my couch, drinking beer, smoking weed, and daydreaming about how rich I was going to be. That qualified as just a normal afternoon for me, except for the subject of my daydreams. Usually my weed-and-beer-inspired fantasies involved women, not money.

At one point I retrieved my old gym bag and spent about a half-hour cleaning the dust off it. It looked almost new when I'd finished, which made a lot of sense considering I'd only used it to go to the gym about three times. Just another one of my great ideas that didn't pan out. Going to the gym, I mean.

When five o'clock rolled around, my stomach started sending me 'I'm hungry' messages – basically just a series of extremely loud groans, grunts, and grumbles telling me it was time to eat – so I grabbed a Hungry Man turkey dinner from my freezer, popped it into the microwave and ate it along with some cranberry sauce. Yum, yum – just like Thanksgiving dinner.

As seven-thirty grew closer, my anxiety level started to rise. For most of the weekend and earlier today I'd felt pretty good. Once I'd finally managed to get into Kozy Keeps and rent a locker, my uneasy feelings had faded away, replaced by dreams of riches. But now they were back. I could sense them, gathering out there in the darkness, getting ready to attack.

I decided to pass on my usual after-dinner smoke, since weed seems to amplify my feelings of anxiety and paranoia. Especially paranoia. A clear head was what I needed to successfully complete my mission.

Oh, stop it! said my little voice.

Stop what?

Stop acting like you're trying to break into CIA headquarters. You're just going to visit a storage facility a few blocks away from here. It's not that big a deal.

Well, it is a big deal. There's money in that locker, I'm sure of it. Maybe millions.

Or not. Just relax. Wait and see. There won't be any problems. You're a member, you have a key. You'll go in, open Buttaree's locker and see what's in there, then decide what to do about it.

But there could be other people there.

So what? They don't know what your locker number is, or Buttaree's, either. And what's more, they don't care about what you're doing – they've got their own situations to deal with.

I knew my little voice was right but knowing it and dealing with it were not exactly the same. Anxiety had been a problem for me since, … well, since I was a little kid. And it wasn't as if I could control it – it came and went on its own schedule, sometimes seeming to be totally unconnected to things happening in my life at the time.

Whatevahs. This part of the plan was going down tonight. And a little anxiety wasn't going to stop it. It was almost seven-thirty. I took a couple of deep breaths, changed into some clean clothes, grabbed my gym bag and left to go meet Kimo.

Chapter Twenty-Eight

Monday evening

Kimo was waiting for me, double-parked on Ohua. Although he'd likely be unwilling to admit it, he suffers from a life-long fear of being late. 'Suffers' probably isn't the right word, but he's always early – sometimes by a lot. I'd be willing to bet he's been out here, waiting for me, for at least 10 minutes. Maybe more.

"Hey," I said as I climbed in. I stored my gym bag on the floor, between my feet, and we headed down Ohua toward Kuhio Avenue.

"What's in the bag?" Kimo said.

"Some old clothes."

"Yeah? Just clothes?"

"Yup."

"So, what's with all the James Bond stuff, anyway?"

As we turned left at Kuhio, I twisted around in my seat and looked through the back window to make sure we weren't being followed. "Just being careful," I told him.

"You gonna tell me what's going on or what?"

"Yeah. I just didn't want to talk about it on the phone."

"So, ...?"

"First, I got a question."

"Okay. Shoot."

"It's hypothetical."

"Ooh, big word. So what is it?"

"What would you do if you found, like, say ... a half-million dollars? In cash."

He gave me a funny look. "Uhh, ... rent out a hotel and throw a party?"

I laughed and said, "C'mon, I'm serious."

"I don't know. I guess I'd share it with you. Give you half."

"Really? You'd give me half?" That was an answer I hadn't expected.

"Yeah. That was the deal we made, back in school. Don't you remember? Share and share alike."

"You're kidding! We were like, what? Ten years old? And that was about candy and comic books, not money."

"Oh, I thought it was about everything."

"Share everything? Does that mean you're going to let me sleep with Kelly?"

"Well, almost everything," Kimo said with a grin.

"So, after you give me half – and thank you very much for that – you've still got a quarter mil, right? What are you going to do with it?"

"I dunno. I've never really thought much about being rich."

"So think about it now. What would you do?"

"Found money, huh? You have to pay taxes, right?"

"Not if you don't tell anybody about it."

"Maybe I'd start a business."

"Yeah? What kind?"

"Haven't got a clue."

"Won't you just inherit Pops' business someday?"

"Yeah, that's the plan. His plan. Leave the business to me."

"What about Pua?" Pua was Kimo's older sister.

"She doesn't want it. She helps Pops with the books but she's not really interested in running the business. To tell you the truth, I'm not sure I want to do it, either."

"No?"

"No. It's boring."

A period of silence ensued, which I eventually broke. "You ever hear of a place called Kozy Keeps Mini-Lockers?" I said.

"Sure. There's a bunch of them, all over the island. There's one on Kapahulu."

"That's where I'm going – the one on Kapahulu."

"Why?"

"I've got a locker there."

He gave me a quizzical look. "That's it? That's what all this secrecy is about? You visiting your locker?"

"Buttaree had a locker there, too."

"Oh. So, ... what? You're going to break into her locker?"

"I don't have to break in. I have a key."

"Really?"

"Yeah."

"And that's where she stashed the money?"

"I dunno. Maybe. I don't know what's in it."

"Where'd you get the key?"

"I found it. The night I searched her apartment." We turned left on Kapahulu and I checked behind us again. As far as I could tell, no one was following us.

"I thought you gave the stuff you found to the cops."

"I gave them the flash drive. But I kept the key."

"Pretty sneaky. They didn't search you?"

"Actually, no. I gave them the flash drive right away and told them that's what I found. I never mentioned the key. I guess they just assumed that was it – the flash drive was all I found."

"So what's your plan? You gonna take the money out of Buttaree's locker and then put it in yours?"

"Something like that. If it's the money. If it's dirty laundry or something, I'm just gonna leave it."

Kimo chuckled. "Yeah, smart. Be careful you don't leave any fingerprints on her locker."

I hadn't thought about that. Although I doubted the police would be checking Kozy Keeps' locations anytime soon, since they had no idea that's where the missing money could be, there was no reason to take unnecessary chances. It wouldn't do to have my fingerprints found on Buttaree's locker.

"Kaimuki Avenue's coming up," Kimo said. If the light's red, you can jump out when I stop. If it's green, I'll turn and drop you off around the corner."

"Okay."

The light was red, so I grabbed my bag and hopped out when he stopped. "Thanks for the lift," I told him.

"You need a ride home?"

"Nah, I'm good. I'll call you, later. Let you know what I found."

"Great."

The light changed to green. I slammed the car door shut and watched Kimo drive away, up toward Waialae Avenue and Kaimuki town. When the light changed again, I crossed Kapahulu and headed down the sidewalk toward Kozy Keeps.

So far, my anxiety level had been at a reasonable level. But as I approached my destination, a sour feeling began to form in the pit of my stomach and that level began to rise. I gulped air and forced myself to continue walking until I was standing in front of the entrance.

You can do this, my little voice encouraged me.

You're right, buddy. I can do this. I took a deep breath, exhaled, and pulled the door open.

A bored-looking young woman sat on a stool behind the counter, chewing gum and scrolling through her phone. "Help you?" she said, looking up as I entered.

I held up my key, which was now on my key ring, having replaced Buttaree's. Her key – the key to locker 31 – was loose in my pocket.

"You got ID?"

"Sure." I reached into my back pocket for my wallet.

"Never mind." She punched the button under the counter and the door to the locker collection popped open.

"Thanks," I said, sliding my wallet back into my pocket.

"We close at nine," she reminded me.

I checked my watch. Twenty to eight. "I won't be that long."

"Excellent," she said, and went back to scrolling through her phone.

I went in and closed the door behind me. No one else was in the room – that's good, I thought. About halfway down the aisle, on the left, I found Buttaree's locker. And mine, too, right next to it. Both of them were on the second level, meaning there was another level of lockers beneath them. That put Buttaree's and mine at a comfortable working height.

So far I had managed to keep my anxiety pretty much in check, but as I stood there, staring at the steel door in front of me, a wave of panicky feelings began sweeping over me. It felt like the early stages of a full-blown panic attack. Having had this experience before – many times, in fact – I knew what to do. I took several deep breaths and waited for it to pass, which it eventually did, leaving me only slightly anxious.

C'mon, c'mon, don't be such a wuss. You can do this.

You're right, buddy. I can.

I placed my bag on the floor, put the key in the lock and turned it, careful not to touch the locker itself. For a minute or so I stood there just looking at the steel door in front of me, unable to open it as another wave of anxiety – smaller this time – swept over me. I waited until it had passed, then took one more deep breath, exhaled and, using the tail of my shirt to avoid leaving fingerprints, opened the locker.

Chapter Twenty-Nine

I don't know what I expected to see when I opened Buttaree's locker, but a shopping bag from an upscale California department store was not it. But that's what was sitting in there, all alone, looking sad and forlorn in the middle of a locker that was way too big for it. I briefly wondered if bags had feelings – I knew some people believed everything, even inanimate objects like shopping bags, had souls. If that was true, the bag in Buttaree's locker – locked up in here, all alone, for who knows how long – was probably glad to see me.

Concentrate! Concentrate on what you're doing!

Right. I returned to the task at hand.

This wasn't one of those paper grocery bags like you can still get at some supermarkets. It was bigger and made of shiny plastic, not paper. It also had cord handles for easy carrying. For a shopping bag, it was fairly impressive. Still, it was disappointing. How much money could you stuff into a shopping bag, anyway? Not much, was my guess.

I stood there, gazing at the shopping bag for a moment or two, then reached in and pulled it toward the front of the locker and looked inside. Staring back at me was a folded sweatshirt with palm trees and the word Hawai'i emblazoned across the front. Not money. That was discouraging.

It isn't likely that Buttaree would rent a locker just to store sweatshirts, noted my little voice. *Let's see what else is in the bag.*

Being careful not to touch the locker, I grabbed the bag by the handles, removed it and locked the locker. Then I took the bag down to the end of the room, where three tables waited for those who wished to examine the contents of their lockers in private. After choosing the table on the left, I placed the shopping bag on it and my gym bag on the floor and pulled the curtains closed.

I took a deep breath, exhaled and removed the apparently-new, never-worn sweatshirt from the bag. Probably a gift for someone was my guess. And under the sweatshirt was ... another sweatshirt, identical to the first!

I took that one out, too. And there it was, staring up at me from the bag – the missing money. Lots of it, too, it looked like. Although technically, I guess, the term missing money no longer applied, since at least one person – me – knew where it was.

First making sure the curtains were securely closed, I dumped it all out onto the table and examined it. It appeared to be entirely composed of hundred-dollar bills, neatly divided into small packs about a half-inch thick and wrapped around the middle with a band of wide yellow paper. And on each yellow band someone had written $10,000 in black ink. I picked up one of the packs, ripped it open and counted the bills in it, laying them out in rows of ten. When I was finished, a hundred portraits of Benjamin Franklin stared up at me from the table. Ten thousand dollars, just as the writing on the yellow band had promised!

I spent the next 10 minutes counting and recounting the money. Then I counted it one more time, just to make sure I hadn't made a mistake. Each time I came up with the same total – $1,478,800. One hundred and forty-seven packs of hundred-dollar bills, plus one other pack, folded in half, consisting of 88 bills.

It was surprising how little room the cash took up in the bag. No one encountering that innocent-looking shopping bag would ever suspect it could easily hold that much money. Plus two extra-large sweatshirts. Earlier, when I thought a bag this size couldn't hold very much cash ... well, I was wrong. Totally wrong.

My fingers were trembling as I put two packs of the money to one side and carefully loaded the rest of it back into the shopping bag. I gazed down at it, all neatly lined up so that it fit almost perfectly into the bag and looking perfectly content to be there. I should have been happy, right? Even ecstatic. But the thought that popped into my head as I stood there looking down at all those beautiful Franklins was not one of joy, but of anxiety – what the hell was I going to do with all this cash?

Don't worry about it, piped up my little voice. *I'm sure we'll think of something.*

I placed the two sweatshirts on top of the cash and stowed the bag inside my gym bag, on top of my old clothes. The two packs of cash that hadn't gone into the bag went into the front pockets of my shorts – one pack in the left pocket, the other in the right. A quick glance around to make sure I hadn't dropped a bill or two showed my work area to be clean and without any stray material that could come back to haunt me in, say, a criminal trial. Satisfied, I took my gym bag over to locker number 30 – my locker – put it inside, locked it and left.

Outside, on the sidewalk in front of Kozy Keeps, I took several deep breaths to calm myself. A rather large amount of anxiety and paranoia had returned. It was difficult not to think that everyone – people on the sidewalk, drivers traversing Kapahulu Avenue, everyone – knew what was going on and that I was now, thanks to a ginormous stroke of good luck, in possession of these ill-gotten gains.

Of course, what was good luck for me had been bad luck for Buttaree, and I felt bad about that. At the same time, though, I'm sure she would have preferred I end up with the cash, rather than Harry Dick or the two goons who killed her. And if I turned the cash over to the cops, probably no one would ever claim it and eventually they'd get it. Better me than any of them, I decided.

I set off down the sidewalk toward Waikiki. As I walked along, putting distance between myself and Kozy Keeps, my anxiety and paranoia seemed to lessen. Had I actually pulled this off? Was I really going to get away with it? Just to make doubly-sure, I turned around and checked behind me. The sidewalk had thinned out and none of the few people I could see seemed to be following me. No cars trailed slowly along behind, stalking me, waiting to pull up onto the sidewalk and trap me while armed men jumped out and forced me into the back seat.

That would be exciting, chimed in my little voice.

But not the good kind of excitement, I argued back.

Whatevahs. Good, bad, who cares? You know what? We're rich!

Yeah. That part was correct. We were rich!

A smile spread slowly across my face, growing larger and more confident with each step I took until, by the time I came to Date Street, it had grown so large it had completely obscured my head. When the light changed and I crossed the street, people were leaning out their car windows and saying things like, "Did you see that?" and, "Hey, wasn't that the Cheshire Cat from that Disney flick?"

Okay, I made that last part up. Obviously, a person's smile cannot be larger than their head. But that's how I felt – like a million bucks worth of happy!

As I skipped down the sidewalk – figuratively, not literally – alongside the Ala Wai Golf Course, I imagined my dad was out there, playing, and what I'd do if I saw him. Of course, that couldn't be. It was night and the course was closed. But in one's imagination, anything is possible, so I imagined myself taking the packs of money out of my pockets, waving them in the air at my dad, and yelling, "Hey, Dad! Guess what? I'm rich!"

For some reason, that fantasy made me feel especially good. But then my dad hollered back, "Go back to school! Get your degree!" and hit a seven-iron to about 15 feet from the pin.

Nice shot, Dad. Apparently, not all fantasies work out the way they were intended. I continued down Kapahulu, feeling better and better with each step I took. All the anxiety and paranoia that had been badgering me for the past few days now seemed gone, replaced by joy and wonderment – joy because of all the money I'd discovered and wonderment because, so far at least, I'd successfully pulled off this little caper.

By the time I reached Ala Wai Boulevard, though, I had discovered that joy and wonderment can be short-lived. A new set of worries had crept into my head. How was I going to explain where I got all this money? And what was I going to do with it? I couldn't put it in the bank. Even though I'd been doing business at the same Kapahulu branch for years and most of the people there knew me, they'd certainly be suspicious if I dropped that much cash on the counter and said, "I'd like to make a deposit."

And I sure didn't want to leave the money at Kozy Keeps. That place was less secure than my apartment. For all I knew, an employee might search the lockers every night after they closed – I'm sure they had a master key or something like that. If that was so, my money would probably be gone the next time I visited it. The sign on the wall – NOT RESPONSIBLE FOR LOST OR STOLEN ITEMS – flashed into my head, as if to remind me.

You know, you're being ridiculous. None of that is likely to happen.
I can't help it. I'm a worrier.
I've got something for you to worry about – something real.
What?
Kimo.
What's he got to do with it?
Share and share alike.
Oh. Yeah.
And Buttaree, too.
Buttaree? But she's dead.
It was her money.
Yeah, so?

She'd probably want her family to get some.

I thought about that for a while as I walked along the wide sidewalk. The canal was to my right and Ala Wai Boulevard – two lanes of one-way traffic going in my direction – was to my left. Paoakalani – my street – was about three blocks up and, although there was a crosswalk nearby, it was dark out and getting cars to stop as they zipped along was always a problem. I decided to just wait for a break in the traffic and jaywalk across the street.

I've got it, I told my little voice.

Got what?

What to do with the money. I'm gonna keep a million and send the rest to Buttaree's family. Then I'm gonna split the million with Kimo. Half a mil each.

That's pretty generous.

Share and share alike, that's the deal.

That's right. Share and share alike. We're still going to have to find a place to keep our share, though.

Yeah, I'll worry about that later.

I looked behind me and saw a break in traffic coming so I reached into my right front pocket, wiggling past the pack of bills, and pulled out the loose locker key – the one to Buttaree's locker – and, pretending it was a Frisbee, I flung it out into the middle of the canal. Since they only clean the canal about every 50 years, it was probably safe to say that it would be a while before anyone found the key, if ever. Not that it made any difference – there was nothing in the locker, anyway.

When the break in the traffic appeared, I sprinted across Ala Wai Boulevard and trotted the remaining two blocks home. I felt great. The anxiety I'd been feeling earlier – actually, for the past couple of weeks – was nowhere around. For once in my life, things had worked out in my favor and I was ready to begin my new life as a rich guy!

That's it, folks. Hope you enjoyed this first book in the *Archie and Kimo* series. If you did, I'd sure appreciate it if you'd leave a review. Thanks for reading.

Chet